THE WINTERING

THAW

Stephen Bowkett was born and brought up in a mining valley in South Wales. He taught English at secondary school in Leicestershire for many years before becoming a full-time writer, and a qualified hypnotherapist. He has published over thirty books, mainly science fiction and fantasy, for both adults and children. He also writes poetry, plays and educational non-fiction.

Thaw is the third and final part of The Wintering, a major trilogy. You can learn more about the world of The Wintering, and check out Steve's other books, by visiting his website:

www.sbowkett.freeserve.co.uk

Also by Steve Bowkett

Dreamcastle
Dreamcatcher

in The Wintering *trilogy*

Ice
Storm

THE WINTERING

THAW

STEPHEN
BOWKETT

Dolphin Paperbacks

First published in Great Britain in 2002
as a Dolphin paperback
by Orion Children's Books
a division of the Orion Publishing Group Ltd
Orion House
5 Upper St Martin's Lane
London WC2H 9EA

A catalogue record for this book
is available from the British Library

Typeset at The Spartan Press Ltd, Lymington, Hants

Printed in Great Britain by
Clays Ltd, St Ives plc

ISBN 1 85881 875 3

As to what happened next, it is possible to maintain
That the hand of heaven was involved,
And also possible to say that when men are desperate
No one can stand against them.

Xenophon

Contents

1

Cold Slaughters

A vast explosion rolled out towards the horizons, destroying the centre of Thule.

The blast-wave arrived seconds later, a tide overwhelming the woodland. Kell saw the trees lashing about like reeds, and the drengs and his thoughts and all that existed were blown away like leaves on a welcoming wind.

Time passed, and after the dust came a silence that settled just as gently on the land. Kell saw nothing of it. He lay unconscious until the protective field of the *Skymaster* relinquished its grip and withdrew like the arms of a mother who knows that her children are safe. A cool breeze blew across the water and this at last chilled the boy so that he shivered and opened his eyes . . .

A sheer wall loomed above him, bulging out like the belly of a giant. Kell was surprised to note that this cliff was made from dark metal plates or facets linked in a wonderful symmetry. Way above, beyond the horizon of this immense and miraculous construction, thin clouds streamed by on a quickening wind. And now the sounds of the landscape returned: some birdsong, the rush of the breeze through the grass, water lapping gently on a nearby shoreline – and the quietly efficient whine of a mechanism which swung one or perhaps more of the facets aside. A moment later, a black sphere appeared out of the wall. It may have been a small object close up, or something much larger and much further away. Kell's mouth hung open at the sight. But he had the very clever insight that the vast structure beneath whose overhang he lay sheltered was probably a similar sphere, but bigger than a hearth-hall – maybe bigger than a town!

Up until now, Kell had simply been intrigued by these strange goings-on. He had felt safe; or rather, the idea of danger had not entered his head. Suddenly however the floating ball dropped directly towards him. He squealed, struggled to move and discovered his weakness and pain.

'Keep away! Don't touch me!'

'Don't be silly, Kell,' said a voice from out of the orb. It was a tantalisingly familiar voice, but heavy with the weight of momentous events. 'We'll fetch you inside. There is a great deal to discuss.'

The boy's wits gathered reluctantly, as though some part of him did not wish to fathom how the world worked. He was truly astonished when a lean silver wulf appeared, and a pretty fair-haired girl, and a bald-headed man who walked with a stick.

The man knelt stiffly beside him and checked Kell's body for injury. 'Bruised,' he said – it was the voice that had come from the orb – 'but otherwise unhurt. Come along Fenrir, Sebalrai. Let's get him aboard . . .'

And only upon hearing their names did Kell start to sob with the unbearable knowledge of what he had done.

Skjebne sent a small swarm of eye orbs to scour the ruins. 'Well!' he muttered, as a cluster of the devices swept in over the centre of the enclave. 'Wierd has been kind to us, I think.' His face was set in a mask of fierce triumph. 'Do you not see the miracle that has happened here?'

Kell shook his head dumbly. The girl Sebalrai took hold of his hand and squeezed it as though to share the good news. And the little man-bat, Tsep, a recent companion, tapped the viewscreen with a tiny black claw and nodded, his face alight with an uncomfortably predatory smile.

'Perhaps the companion orb understood its fate,' Skjebne speculated. 'However it was, it has plunged down through the decayed core of the city – surely destroying the weorthan matrix, but leaving most of the outskirts intact.'

Indeed, things could have been much worse. Once the physical shock of the explosion had ebbed and Kell came back to his senses, he expected to find total devastation where Thule once stood. But here before him lay a tumbled panorama of buildings, all damaged but many still standing; people picking about among the semi-ruins and, here and there, making an end of the Tarazad drengs that had survived. The little group watching from a distance also saw human bodies, and Kell forced himself to look so that the memory would stay with him; so that he would never forget that all of this was his responsibility.

'Much of the central city was under-eaten by tunnels,' Skjebne went on, a fact that Kell remembered well enough. 'The vast weight of the plummeting orb collapsed Helcyrian's domain upon itself . . .'

As though to verify his theory he sent two eye orbs soaring down into the pit, their onboard searchlights picking out the slowly twisting veils of smoke and dust that lifted up gently from the depths through the heat of the fires that burned below.

Nothing could be alive down there, commented Fenrir. His

picture-words were clear and bright in Kell's head. *The evil of Thule has ended.*

'I think enough has been done to assure that,' Skjebne agreed once Kell had passed on the wulf's thoughts. The eye orbs moved carefully through the murk, each a feature of the other's viewpoint. They were going ever more slowly now, for great slabs of masonry and spars of steel and other debris clogged the pit in every direction and the smoke was thickening by the second.

Presently Skjebne leaned back in his seat, satisfied.

'All right. I will call them back. There is nothing more to be seen. If any weorthan remains intact it is buried deep under. And therefore Helcyrian herself must surely be gone.'

He gave the command and the watchers turned their attention to the other screens – and to one in particular a minute later, which showed three burly warriors covered in grime carrying the unconscious body of Hora, their battle-brother.

'Well, I won't be picking any fights with *you* in the future, young Kell.' Hora sat slumped in a towelled robe nursing his forehead in one hand and a whole juggon of meodu in the other. The dust and mud were washed from him leaving his hair and beard the startling scarlet of the Wyrda Craeftum; the dye could never be removed and was a mark of his commitment. His three companions, Alef, Myrgen and Thoba laughed at his grumpiness. They had not been buried under a collapsing fruit wain and so could afford easy mirth at his expense. Besides, it helped to conceal the memory of the terror that had gripped them all to their bones.

'I could not think of any other way. And I didn't want to say too much about my plan, or even give it much thought. If Helcyrian had anticipated our attack, none of us would have lived.'

'I agree,' Thoba said. 'Given that your intention was to wipe out the sorceress I think you went about it sensibly—'

'Sensibly!' Hora swigged at his liquor and wiped his mouth roughly with his fist. He glared at his kinsman and then at the boy. 'You could have brought doom down on us all. Apart from which, you destroyed one of the Great Orbs of the Craeftum.'

'We still have this one . . .' It was a weak response and Kell knew it. Although the action had cut him inside more deeply than any wound, and although he must live forever with its consequences, he felt strong and sound and sure. Fenrir knew it – he could smell the musk of his friend's confidence and realised that Hora was now more frighten-ed of Kell than of Thule's devastation.

'That's hardly the point. You had no right.'

'But I had the ability,' Kell replied quietly, 'and I had the imagination.'

'It could have been worse –'

The door had slid open and Skjebne stood at the threshold. He smiled a little tiredly but warmly at Kell. 'The lad might have possessed the ability but *no* imagin-ation. Now that would be a dangerous thing indeed.'

'Yes but –'

'We could go on arguing backwards and forwards like a gaggle of *ealdmodoren* at their looms.' Skjebne used the comparison deliberately to lighten the mood. 'It is of little importance how we feel. We are guided by Wierd all alike, and Wierd brought Kell and the sky orbs together and put

Helcyrian in their way. Now the boy has proven himself to a greater authority than you or I, Hora . . . Although Thorbyorg has a few words to say on the matter. He has sent a message which the *Skymaster's* mind received and passed on to me. We must return to Uthgaroar now.'

'For my punishment?' Kell wondered calmly. It all seemed so pointless being ordered around by these men!

They act for the greater good, as you do, Fenrir interjected. The boy's thoughts were as bright as a flashing swordblade. *Never make the mistake of arrogance, whatever part you play in Wierd's game.*

It was sound counsel and Kell let his anger settle. He looked into the wulf's clear intelligent yellow eyes and offered up thanks and respect.

'I don't think punishment comes into it,' Skjebne said. 'The loss of life at Thule was largely confined to the dreng swarms – and philosophers could argue long over the sense in which they were alive. As for the loss of the Orb, Thorbyorg rejoices in the existence of this one. And as you have said Kell, there are surely others out there but for the finding of them.'

'Then why do we return to Uthgaroar?'

'Thorbyorg was not clear in his request. I had the impression that significant things were happening there.' He glanced mischievously across at Hora. 'And I think he wants your opinion about them.'

Before Kell gave the command to send *Skymaster* on its way, he had the orb hang in the sky above the shattered ruins of Thule. To the people below the appearance of the great ball of iron was a favourable omen, but Kell just wanted to be sure the danger was over.

'They have enough food and fuel.' Skjebne rested his

hand on Kell's shoulder. 'And the warmer season is imminent.' They stood together in the crystal room and it was as though they floated free in the air above the city. The last of the little eye orbs were speeding up from the four quarters to nestle in the *Skymaster's* hull. 'Not one of them has seen a dreng moving. Besides, most of these people are travellers. They know how to survive in the open.'

Kell smiled. 'You have done your best to reassure me, Skjebne. And you have succeeded. I promise I will not regard myself as a murderer now.'

The boy sent out a thought and the ship responded instantly. The city dropped away until it looked like a little bowl between the jumbled grey hills, hazy with smokes and the low light of the afternoon sun. Then the whole world swung aside as the orb pivoted round and soared in an elegant arc towards the west.

The sturdy buildings of Uthgaroar were picked out in white. Snow had come and been quickly scoured away by the endless winds, save for the dry ice dust that lodged in corners and along the leeward edges of walls. The blue-white smoke of hearth fires was visible afar off, streaming away to nothingness among the night's early stars. Higher up, between the settlement and the bleak tops, some *generan* had been busy that afternoon piling and tending a beacon fire to guide the *Skymaster* home. Skjebne smiled at the *naïveté* of the act; it would be like telling a veteran warrior how to handle a sword.

'We are here,' he said as he stood alone in the crystal room, and his voice was conveyed at once throughout the ship to all of its occupants.

7

Soon afterwards, when the travellers were sensibly clothed against the cold, Skjebne commanded the hatchway to open. A short distance below and sheltered by the rocks, Thorbyorg himself and a retinue of wyrda warriors stood waiting to greet the arrivals.

'We have food and *wyrtegemang* ready!' the First Eolder bellowed above the lean whining of the wind, and laughed with pleasure at seeing his friends safely returned.

They walked together down the narrow hill path to the hearth hall – save for Skjebne who, despite his protestations, was carried by two sturdy *generan*.

'You'd freeze else with the time it would take you,' Thorbyorg pointed out seriously. 'Then what use would you be to anyone!'

'Yes, yes, yes,' Skjebne grumbled. Even so he felt this was an indignity and determined then to do something about it.

The journey was brief, however, and Skjebne was set down when they arrived outside the gathering place. Thorbyorg burst in with his guests to the cheers of the people: the celebrations had already, clearly, begun. Immediately warriors and commonfolk alike surrounded the group, eager to talk with them or just be close to these heroes returning in victory from such an impossible battle. Skjebne was fully in his element and relished the attention, but Tsep crawled into a deep pouch inside Kell's tunic, while Fenrir chose to join Magula and his wulfen pack away from the bustle. Even Sebalrai, who had gained so much in confidence since Feoh and Kell had found her, looked alarmed.

She whispered to Kell. 'I am so proud of you . . . But I thought from what Skjebne said that Thorbyorg would be furious with the destruction of the sky orb . . .'

'This reaction surprises me too,' Skjebne said. He had been eavesdropping without shame. 'I will ask over its significance . . .' And he did so, and the First Eolder broke off from the merriment and put a more serious cast on his face.

'The people rejoice over what might have been, but through your action was not. If Helcyrian had lived then her dreng swarm would be marching towards Uthgaroar even now. That will never happen. But more importantly,' Thorbyorg continued, leaning closer, 'there have been changes in the Wheel. Deep changes, Kell, caused we are sure by what has occurred. I meant to explain these matters later, but if you are concerned by not knowing then let us deal with them now.'

Thorbyorg gave some brief instructions to Garulf, his assistant, and then led Kell and Skjebne away. Kell turned to reassure Sebalrai that he would be back very soon but she was nowhere to be seen – though she had not gone, for a second later he felt her small hand slide into his and he smiled at the elegance and usefulness of her gift of veiling.

The First Eolder took them to a quiet chamber not far from the main hall. It was a dark private place and the air was heavy with the smoke of sweet resin and a sense of reverence. Firetar torches burned sombrely within stone niches set in the walls, while between them hung draperies of black cloth decorated with the same sigils and symbols that the wyrda men tattooed on their bodies.

In the centre of the room stood a stout oak table varnished and polished until it glowed with a red-black sheen. Chairs of wrought steel were positioned around, and in these sat six stony-faced eoldermen staring silently at the Universal Wheel nestling on a base of carven crystal.

'This is the room of decisions,' Thorbyorg announced with a subtle edge of irony in his voice that at least Kell noticed, but which seemed to pass the eoldermen by. 'This is where we discern the Wierd of our people as it is configured in the Wheel, and then act upon what the oracle has told us.'

Skjebne glanced sidelong at Kell, but the boy was mature enough not to smirk. For many generations the Wheel had been all but inactive, its nested rings unmoving and dumb. Only recently after Skjebne repaired one of the eye orbs in his workroom at Edgetown had any significant changes begun. Shortly after that, when Kell's mind joined with the spirit of the Wheel, the *Skymaster* came at his bidding and the long vigil of the Wyrda Craeftum was over.

'So what is the oracle telling you now?' Skjebne wanted to know. The assembled eoldermen stirred uneasily and Thorbyorg cleared his throat but said nothing. Skjebne let the silence linger, allowing his audience to understand that he was poorly impressed by their manner.

'Do you *know* what it is telling you now?' He went on with a gentle insistence, looking at each of the dignitaries in turn though none of them would meet his eye. 'Surely at the very least the Wheel is signalling that the events of the past moon are a *minor* thing when set against the resources the wyrda possess!'

Kell was intrigued to see the shock register on the faces of these old men who had for years maintained their positions in the clan through a sham of wisdom and inaction. They had sat here and watched the tiny shiftings of the rings and agreed great meanings among themselves. But all the while, Kell thought, all the while they had not been truly open to the Wheel's teachings and to its power.

'Look here!' Skjebne startled them all. He walked to the table, leaned over and audaciously tapped at the Wheel with his finger. One eolder, a thin-faced man with a pointed white beard, grew flushed with rage but still didn't speak, afraid as he was to be carried away by new and unknown circumstances.

'If I remember how the Wheel looked last time I saw it – I notice now that *this* ring has turned a minimal degree . . . And *this* one has spun round a finger-width . . . Oh, and here are some tiny glimmerings which I think were not there before . . .'

'That, by and large, is correct,' Thorbyorg said a little stiffly.

'So what about the rest of the rings? Why have they not moved? And why is the whole Wheel not ablaze with light? Why – because even though we have use of the *Skymaster*, even though its companion was destroyed in smashing Helcyrian, the power contained in the Wheel has barely been tapped!'

'If I may add to that please.' Kell stepped forward to address the assembly directly. 'Undoubtedly my friend Skjebne is right. When *Skymaster* took us to the plateau where it had rested since, perhaps, before the Ice, we found not only its companion but also a third platform. Its orb was missing, but quite clearly three orbs once existed there. And I wondered then, as I wonder now, whether that nesting place is but one of many scattered across the world? We command the *Skymaster*. We can seek them out.'

The thin-faced man in his rage spoke at last.

'How can a child presume to come here and tell us –'

'Leofsonu,' Thorbyorg said warningly. 'Do not compound your error with unthinking anger. Let the boy speak.'

'Thank you First Eolder. The fact that my childhood stands beside me and not at arm's length means that I am not frightened of these great possibilities. I am awed by the *Skymaster* but not cowed by it. In a sense it is just like a *genera*.'

'Oh, hardly.' Leofsonu almost spat the word.

'It is a servant,' Kell insisted. 'It was built by human hands to fulfil human purposes . . . Very well then, if you object to *Skymaster* finding others of its kind, why don't we use it to achieve the destiny of the wyrda? Why don't we follow the Sigel Rad now – immediately – all of us here in this room!'

And now neither Skjebne nor Thorbyorg could keep the smiles from their faces. Here was the youth challenging these men to leave their seats and climb aboard the orb and be taken into the heavens – perhaps to the glorious starhoard that the Eye of the Rad depicted. It was too huge a prospect, too terrifying a dare. Was the *Skymaster* indeed even capable of such a feat? Skjebne considered this before the assurance *that it could* came into his mind and humbled him.

It was Kell's turn to use silence to his advantage. Without giving the matter any thought (deliberately so, for his feelings were truer than his ponderings) he reached between Leofsonu and his neighbour and lifted the Wheel off its base. Several eoldermen swallowed back their protests and outrage, but no one rose up to stop him.

'Let us learn to dream, gentlemen, so that we will know the truth.'

And though Kell said nothing more and certainly did not manipulate the Wheel in his hands, several exterior rings moved and circled and twinkled suddenly with a play of tiny lights.

The eoldermen stared around themselves as though the world was ending.

'What have you done?' Leofsonu demanded. 'Your meddling could kill us all!'

'My meddling saved you from the drengs,' Kell pointed out. 'As to what I have done; well, I put my faith in Wierd and wait to see what tomorrow will bring.'

And at that he replaced the Wheel on its crystal base, inclined his head politely to the people he had so thoroughly horrified and smartly left the room.

'". . . I put my faith in Wierd and wait to see what tomorrow will bring." And then he walked out!' Skjebne's face was already flushed from too much *meodu* and the roaring hearth hall fires. Now he erupted into laughter and rocked back on his seat. If Hora had been in a less apprehensive mood he might have grabbed Skjebne to stop him tipping over. As it was, Sebalrai's quick action saved the day.

'You're drunk you old *gat*! I don't find the amusement that you do in any of this. It isn't funny,' Hora said.

But Sebalrai was smiling, albeit more at Kell's embarrassment, while Tsep's grin might have been one of mirth, but nonetheless looked slightly chilling – and hungry.

The little group of them, the close friends, sat apart from the general celebrations that were still going on. There was no sign of Fenrir and the other wulfen: flames and loud laughter and the stink of liquor were not to their liking. They would be settled somewhere outside among the rocks, at home in the night.

'Well the people are happy,' Sebalrai commented with a hint of mischief. 'They seem pleased with what's going on.'

'Aye, well they don't understand the implications. Following the Sigel Rad means leaving everything we have ever known behind. You know, Uthgaroar was built here high in the mountains to be close to heaven. For thousands of moons the people have put up with hardship for that reason. But if you were to suggest to them that now we could actually *go there*, I fear they would shake in their boots. Look at them, they are like the commonfolk of Perth. They are comfortable in their ordinary lives.'

'What of the warriors of the wyrda?' Kell asked. 'Such as yourself, Hora?'

'I would go,' the man replied after a brief pause. He nodded. 'Yes. If I knew that the world was safe from the likes of Helcyrian, then I would be happy to go.'

'Then you are a true wyrda who does not deny his destiny,' Skjebne said, suddenly seeming sober. 'And once you are assured that the All Mother and her Sustren are defeated, I will help you to follow your road.'

Shortly afterwards Kell found that the long day had got the better of him and he excused himself from the company. Thorbyorg had arranged for the best apartments in Uthgaroar to be given over to his guests, and although there was a direct passage from the hearth hall to Kell's comfortable room, he chose instead to walk around the building outside.

As it was on so many nights here, tonight the stars were brilliant and unwinking in the sky and the cold was so intense that it seemed to preserve the moment in a crystal shell so that any loud sound or sudden movement might shatter its perfection.

Kell looked around himself and let his breath out slowly and watched it drift up and up as a pale mist until it was part of the heavens. He had come outside to be away from the heat and stuffiness of the hearth hall, and to seek his wulfen friends. But as it happened every time, so they now found him first without effort.

Peace is all the more precious after conflict, Fenrir said. The young wulf sat atop a rocky point gazing down calmly at his friend. Nearby stood Gauda, the best guard-wulf of the pack, as grey and unmoving as stone.

I prefer this to the revelry inside, Kell admitted. *There is an edge of apprehension in the joy of the people.*

Your insights are accurate I think. Most of these folk are settled with the way things are. I suspect that secretly many hoped that the Sun's Way would never be revealed to them . . . The eoldermen have lived well on it!

Kell smiled and realised that Fenrir must have followed events closely through the boy's own eyes. The wulf's amusement glowed in him for a moment.

Just imagine the outrage if Leofsonu and the rest had been confronted with a female and a fourlegs at their conclave, as well as a youth who offered them some plain hard truths!

Perhaps I feel just a little sorry for them, Kell said, realising it even as the thought came to him. *How easily I might have been just as contented in Perth under Gifu's simple teaching. Accepting it all could be so effortless . . .*

Your blood decided otherwise, Kell. Fenrir sprang down from the rock and landed without sound beside him. *Magula feels that perhaps it was intended that you, or someone like you, should be born into an enduring society like Perth's when the time was right for change. He believes that Wierd had planned your coming.*

Well that may be so. When are we ever truly free to choose?

Kell asked the question without anticipating any answer. For a while he and Fenrir stood together and let the night absorb them, until Gauda stirred at his guard post and sniffed the air curiously.

Do you smell something important, wulfenbrooor? Fenrir wondered without looking round.

Only tomorrow, Gauda replied, and settled back down to his watch.

Later – alone – asleep – Kell dreamed of Feoh. He realised then, even deep in his slumber, that she visited him as a real presence and was not just a ghost of his mind. At first he did not know her, for no longer was she the cold, hard capable fighter she had proved to be in Perth. This Feoh was dressed in airy sylks and wore delicate silver jewellery and was complete of face. When Kell stared, as any man must stare at her beauty, she blushed and was coy and then a little ashamed at her choice of illusion.

No one judges you for wanting that, Kell reassured her. She was as flickering and ephemeral as a butterfly, as though the slightest disturbance would cause her to vanish. *Feoh, are you frightened?*

No more than I have ever been since I left you at Edgetown.

Why – how – what has happened . . . ? His flurry of half-formed questions made her smile.

There isn't time now to tell you in any detail. But be warned that news of Helcyrian's death and the defeat of the Shahini Tarazad has spread quickly. The Sustren and the All Mother who guides them have pledged your destruction.

None of that surprises me. We reasoned that the All Mother was not confined to Perth.

She seeks to be free in the world, Feoh said and momentarily faded before returning like a thought that has come again to mind. *She seeks to be free and will walk any road to achieve this. Shamra has become deeply involved —*

The name struck Kell like a blow.

I have heard rumours of her at Kairos.

Where —

It is too dangerous for you to know it all now. You would come after her.

Of course I would!

And meet your death very quickly. You must go instead to a settlement called Hugauga. I have placed the way in the Sky-master's mind. Once there, find the man called Wrynn. He is one of the Erulian guild, who are Thrall Makers. He can explain more about Kairos and the Sustren and Shamara's part in all of this.

These are strange sounding names . . . But what of you, Feoh?

I endanger myself by coming to you. The Sustren would punish me severely if they found me out.

Are you their prisoner? Can you escape from them?

Perhaps I can, the woman said, and now she was fading completely to become just an echoing thought. *But I am not their prisoner. I* am *Sustren now, Kell. I have bound myself to their ways.*

He woke in the earliest grey light of dawn with his heart beating quickly. For a few confused seconds Kell wondered if the dream had been spun by the All Mother to set him against Feoh, his ally. But then he knew the deeper truth, that the woman had found him and risked her life to tell him these things.

Kell washed himself quickly with icy cold water, dressed, then hurried out to impart his news to Skjebne and the others. Again he chose the outside way, for Fenrir and the wulfen also must know . . .

And after a few steps he stopped short with a gasp of astonishment. The sun was a promised light below the distant peaks, but already the sky glow was strong enough to cast in crisp silhouette the three great orbs that had come here at his bidding as he had held the Universal Wheel the evening before.

2

The Sith

Windhover. Cloudfarer. Heavenwalker. Kell named the three orbs in those first few moments of amazement. Or perhaps it had been something much more profound – *Nemnao hy sylfe.* They name themselves. However it was, the great spheres hung there like dark lamps waiting for his bidding. And Kell smiled to think that in the sacred chamber where the eoldermen met, the Universal Wheel would now be turning and sparkling to reflect the way of Wierd.

It was not long before Gauda had passed the news to Magula and the rest of his pack. A dozen sleek animals loped out of hiding to watch the sun rise between the mountain pinnacles and set the mists in the valley afire and cast crescents of light on the orbs.

The Wheel is awake to your dreams, wulfensweor, Fenrir said. *Surely it must approve of your plans.*

I keep thinking that I am simply fitting in with the greater plan of the Wheel, which is turned like a toy in Wierd's hands. He looked at the wulf who regarded him with eyes of calm amber.

Does it really matter? Fenrir replied. *Is the river the banks or the water between?*

Before very long the first-rising of Thorbyorg's people came from their houses, saw the spectacle of the spheres and spread the word quickly through the settlement – for Uthgaroar had gone unguarded for the first time in generations because of the homecoming celebrations. Thorbyorg himself came hurrying out with gat fur pelt slung hastily over his sleeping clothes. His boots were unlaced and his hair was a straggling thatch of red and grey strands.

'By the Rad, youngling, but you know how to wake a man from his sleep!' The First Eolder squinted up to the heavens and shook his head slowly and let out a trembling breath.

'Just one of these orbs could take Uthgaroar's entire population along the Sun's Way,' said Skjebne who was standing close by. 'The Wierd of your clan can be realised.'

'Well, for those who choose –'

'The time is not yet,' Kell interrupted, apologising a second afterwards. 'Forgive me, but the orbs' arrival is not the only thing that happened in the night . . .' And he went on to tell them of the vision of Feoh and the news that she brought.

'. . . So Helcyrian was just one of the Sustren; a local tyrant. They are spread across the world, from what I understand of the matter. And all are controlled by the Goddess who enfolds them in her warm and brooding wings.' Kell gave a little hard smile of hatred.

'And the enchanter, Wrynn, and the Thrall Makers – what of them?'

'I can tell you only what Feoh told me, Skjebne; or rather what I can remember of it. *Skymaster* knows the way to Hugauga. Wrynn can lead us to Kairos. And from there, I am as ignorant as the rest of us.'

Skjebne chuckled and patted Kell's shoulder. 'At least you freely admit your ignorance, my *frio*.'

'What I am saying is that the Wyrda's part in all of this is not finished. We used two orbs and the skill of the Craeftum to overcome Helcyrian. But to defeat the All Mother herself . . .' He left the rest unsaid as his imagination failed him.

'Our first step is to follow Feoh's advice and seek out the man named Wrynn,' Skjebne said. 'That seems the only sensible way.'

'Well, it is the only way available to us,' Kell added. 'As for the sense of it – remember that we are trusting a dream and the belief that the vision I saw truly was of Feoh.'

Kell's doubt troubled him through the morning, to the extent that he brought the three new orbs close to the earth and boarded each in turn to check for dangers. In this Tsep aided him. The little hreaomus was small and fleet and brave enough to explore the orb's extensive passageways and chambers very quickly. Before the sun had reached the top of its arc that day he was done.

As it was with Skymaster, Tsep said, *so in these others are places where I could not go.*

There were portals locked to you?

Yes Kell. Each orb contains sealed rooms. But at times . . . He showed his tiny needle teeth. *At times I just had the feeling that I should not venture on. Instinct perhaps was warning me away.*

You were right to follow your intuition, Tsep, and I thank you. Kell conveyed all of this to the others. 'So we are no better off. The orbs may still be nothing more than elaborate traps set to tempt us.'

'When *Skymaster* came to us your excitement and joy

were boundless,' Skjebne reminded him. 'What has changed now, Kell?'

'The waters are deeper. The currents are more dangerous.'

'You can still swim, boy,' said Hora who stood a little way off. 'My own time of fear and doubt are still fresh in my mind. In Perth I was a simple fisherman, as you know. When Kano found me he looked to me for strength, but I looked to him for confidence. He helped me greatly in that – but you helped me more. If you distrust the orbs now they will sense it. We all will. Your faith has sustained us, Kell. What use is your vision without it?'

This was a long speech for Hora and a heartfelt one. When it was finished he noticed the faces that were turned towards him and smiled sheepishly and looked at his feet.

'Words well spoken, dear friend!' Skjebne's face was beaming. 'We all walk Wierd's way together. Kell, you are never alone. And now look, we have spent a morning returning to where we started out. The time has come, I think, for us to act.'

Skjebne took charge without any argument, and Kell was glad to find brief peace in the man's shadow. Out of courtesy to the eoldermen of Uthgaroar (Kell could not bring himself to call it respect) a meeting was called in the chamber of the Wheel where the plans for the future could be set.

'. . . And so we propose to leave the three new orbs in position above the settlement,' Skjebne said, having earlier secured Thorbyorg's agreement. 'We have found that all are in communication with each other and with *Skymaster*. And so we will know how you fare, as you will of us. Before we set out, Kell and I will instruct some of your people in the ways of the orbs. Use that learning to learn more by yourselves. Become familiar with the machines. And then, if the call to battle arrives, you can respond swiftly.'

Thorbyorg nodded and gave a heavy sigh.

'We can do no more than follow your advice.' He looked around the table and made sure he caught the eye of every eoldermen in turn. 'At last – at long last – the Sigel Rad is open to us but for this final obstacle. It is time we justified the patience of our ancestors and our own ignorant existence.'

As they had done once before, so the good folk of Uthgaroar loaded up the *Skymaster* with provisions and prepared to say their farewells. Kell had made it clear to them – and Skjebne had endorsed this – that their journey was only an exploration to find Wrynn and discover what he had to tell. This was no serious assault upon the Sustren and the All Mother, for wars were won as much with information as with weapons and men.

'And so our company will be few,' Skjebne added. 'Kell, myself, Sebalrai and Hora, Tsep and Fenrir. Each can bring something to the whole without burden. As a small group we can move quickly –'

'Though hardly without notice,' Thorbyorg said wryly, and believed he was right until Sebalrai somehow twisted thought or light or both and swept the group from the First Eolder's view.

'I stand corrected.' Thorbyorg looked startled when his friends reappeared moments later. If Sebalrai had wanted to, she could have wiped their existence entirely from his mind.

'And by and by we will return, and know what to do for

23

the best.' Skjebne made a respectful bow to all the people of Uthgaroar and boarded the orb with a relish that hardly showed in his eyes. The others followed on once their partings were completed.

It was late in the brief day now and the wind had honed itself on the precipitous cliffs below the settlement. Even so, no one sought out their hearth fires until the *Skymaster* was nothing more than a flickering spark in the evening sky, a minute later extinguished by distance and mist.

The six travellers stood in the crystal room and it was as though they hovered just a few spans above Uthgaroar, with wood smoke drifting past their window. *Cloudfarer* must have taken up position very close to the settlement, and this was the perspective through its eyes. The company laughed to notice how people would come out of their houses every minute or so, just to check that the orbs were still there. And once the wulf called Hyld padded by and sniffed at the air, seeming to realise that he was being watched by folk that he knew.

How interesting it would be, Fenrir speculated, to have an orb controlled by a wulfen mind . . .

You couldn't get one along a forest track, Kell jested, not knowing how serious Fenrir was being.

No, but we could find new forests . . .

And the moment moved on and nothing more was mentioned. But Fenrir felt content that he had placed the seed thought in the slow-eyes' minds.

The night passed without incident. Two of the group at a time took a watch in the crystal room – Hora and Fenrir, Skjebne and Tsep, Kell and Sebalrai – although there was never a doubt that *Skymaster* could look out for itself. Nevertheless, it was an incomparable experience to sit supported by an invisible force and to feel that you were soaring through the sky. The illusion was perfect and complete save for the hatchway entrance to the room which appeared only as a dark space empty of stars. An *almost* perfect illusion like life itself, Kell pondered and thought that was very profound.

For an hour he felt wonderfully settled with Sebalrai nestling beside him, content that their affections were growing in a sure and quiet way without pressure on either of them from the other. That was good, for Kell knew that he was still bound to Shamra by many complex links – not least because he truly loved her – and would not have the whole matter straight in his mind until he saw her again and could talk things through. He thought of her now and what she would be like, six seasons older and tempered by the ordeal of her capture. Maybe she didn't think of him at all; maybe she wouldn't even know him . . . Perhaps, like Feoh, she had joined the Sustren and chosen the All Mother's way . . .

Now Kell had led himself into feeling troubled. He noticed that his arm was numb where Sebalrai was leaning on it and he shifted and disturbed her light slumber.

'You are supposed to be on watch,' he said, intending to be waspish. But her tumbled corn-coloured hair and the sleepy confusion in her eyes took the edge off his mood and he kissed her forehead lightly.

'So . . .' She stretched and yawned and pointed. 'You spotted those already?'

Kell looked where she was looking and saw a cluster of small dark specks speeding away from the orb. At first they

25

followed an identical course but then flew apart on separate trajectories; some soaring up until they caught the light of the still-unrisen sun, others dropping down towards the land's deep darkness.

'Of course I did,' he blustered. 'They are eye orbs that Skjebne has deployed to search in a wide swathe around us.' And by way of confirmation the panorama of the crystal room changed: Kell and Sebalrai were treated to the spectacle of the curved earth spread out below them and a glorious red sun radiating vast veils of light through mountain ridges way up into the sky. A thin crescent moon (the She-Wulf-Claw-Moon, Kell reminded himself) hung like a white shave of ice not a handspan away. And there was another light too, like the brightest star, unmoving close by.

Still the eye orb rose and the platform of the world sank away; the sky lost its blue tinge and turned black; the sun's light grew brighter and clearer and more golden.

'Forgive me.' Skjebne's voice came out of the air itself. 'I could not resist testing the eye orb's capabilities. I hope the sudden change of scene did not startle you.'

'It woke us up,' Kell replied. 'And now I'm awake I am hungry!'

'Hora's preparing some food – go and help him before he smothers everything in powdered *wyrtegemang* and fire sauce. What he relishes can kill ordinary mortals!'

The two did as they were told and joined the others in a small eating room close to the galley. Fenrir was enjoying some strips of raw meat that Hora had thoughtfully but misguidedly cut up for him, while Tsep clung contentedly to a bag that hung from the ceiling. It was made from a gat's bladder filled with the animal's blood.

26

'Drink well little friend,' Kell said and Tsep replied with a red slash of a smile.

They sat to their meal and were pleasantly surprised that the eggs Hora served them were cooked to perfection, as were the slices of ground-fruit moistened with the juice of the *sealt* or savoury nut. Kell ate a second portion, which even so was miniscule compared to the towering pile of breakfast that Hora put out for himself, and promptly proceeded to demolish.

I hope he's left some for Skjebne! Fenrir was cleaning himself after eating and his thoughts were warm and languid with contentment.

'Where is Skjebne anyway?' Kell wanted to know.

'Still in the room of controls I suppose.' Hora spoke through a mouthful and Sebalrai made an expression of disgust.

'Until a minute ago anyway –' Skjebne stood in the doorway, clearly excited to the point of agitation. Kell could see the round black shape of an eye orb hovering patiently behind him.

'Have we come to Hugauga?'

'No, no. I think we are still a quarter-day distant from there. No, the eye orbs have found something else.'

Skjebne stepped into the room and ignored his friends' puzzled looks and the gesture Hora made to the galley where Skjebne's food was cooling. The man seemed to be in mischievous mood as he beckoned the eye orb closer. A number of its screens were glowing, each displaying a view transmitted by one of its fellows. Kell noticed a range of hills draped with a pelt of tall *furhwudu*: and from another screen shone a mountain lake whose dark waters glowed with the glorious opalescence of dissolved minerals. Its neighbour displayed a sky-scape, while the screen next to that . . .

Kell's heart clenched and seemed to swoop down in his chest. He felt the blood leaving his face. Sebalrai turned to him in concern, while Tsep was simply bewildered. All that the screen showed was a range of high peaks above a tumble of scree-littered hills and deep valleys cut through time by fast foaming rivers.

Now Hora also was reacting to the scene. He too looked shocked and the skin around his eyes was taut.

'By the Rad, it can't be!'

But Skjebne's head was moving in a series of little jerking nods. His face was animated.

'Yes – yes. Wierd is playing games with us again. It is Perth.'

They debated the matter at length as *Skymaster* hung unmoving between the mountain pinnacles.

'But what would be the point of going there?' Hora wanted to know. His face showed frustration and disapproval, but Skjebne knew that this simply covered his fear and the dark memories of their escape – Birca's death, the sun's disappearance, the screaming and the flames and the awful retribution of the opticus.

'All experiences are valuable,' Kell said trying to sound wise. His interest lay in seeing Gifu again, to reassure himself that the old landsman had survived.

'Skjebne's stabbing was a valuable thing, then, and the fact that pain is now his constant companion? Oh, and of course we have the priceless experience of Kano's death and Shamra's disappearance –'

'That's enough Hora!' Skjebne's voice cracked out, then

moderated instantly because this was not a time for anger. 'If Kell was entirely wrong we would never have escaped from Perth in the first place. The Community there was so stagnant partly because we took our lives for granted and never thought any experience had value. We simply reacted. Now we can reflect.'

'I still say going back inside serves no purpose and is delaying our mission,' the big warrior said, and folded his huge arms and sat stubbornly silent.

'Well I would agree with you if this thought hadn't occurred to me – How is it that Helcyrian ruled in Thule, but in Perth the All Mother was never to be seen?'

In that wondering, Skjebne won the day. It was a puzzle that intrigued Hora too. 'But you can never go back,' he insisted. 'There can be no going back.'

'We are only returning to a place, not to life as it was.' Kell's voice was gentle and unaccusing. 'Besides, you'd never get into a tavern looking like that!'

But Hora was not to be persuaded. The party talked a while longer, and it was decided that for the reason Skjebne had given Kell, Sebalrai and Fenrir would venture into the enclave – but for no longer than a local day. Hugauga still beckoned and whatever lay in store for them there. The group would have eye orbs to accompany them, so Skjebne's presence would be at their shoulder: Hora and Tsep would also stay aboard *Skymaster* and follow their friends' progress, and avenge their deaths if Hora's darkest fears were realised.

They became quick and efficient in their preparations, and while the sun was still obscured by the fortress of the mountains the three venturers left the warmth and safety of the orb and walked along the pass that Kell remembered so well, until they came to the huge outer doors of the enclave.

'They are as we left them,' Skjebne said from the eye orb that hovered closest by. Two others swept ahead through the freezing mist and disappeared into the chamber beyond the open portals. 'It is safe,' Skjebne confirmed moments later. Sitting in the room of controls aboard *Skymaster*, he was able to influence all of the eye orbs at once and view the world from their multiple perspectives.

The machines give Skjebne good counsel. Fenrir was carefully sniffing the air. *I smell no enemies inside.*

They went on their way, Kell most nervously of the three. He carried the firelance that Hora had offered him. It was a wyrda weapon, and although not as versatile as the multiblade he had once owned, its power was formidable. The same force of apprehension prompted Kell to lend Sebalrai his jewelled knife.

'Can I fight a deity with it?' she'd challenged him gently, but had taken it anyway out of respect for his feelings.

The outrider orbs forged ahead and came first to the high terraces that overlooked the enclave of Perth. 'It looks unchanged,' Skjebne relayed to them, but there was a catch in his voice and Kell noticed that he said nothing further for some time.

Shortly afterwards, with a warm sweet wind flowing into their faces, Kell led Sebalrai and Fenrir to the threshold of what had once been his home. They emerged from the cleft in the rocks and the whole of the world of the enclave was laid out before them, vast and serene.

'Kell . . . It is so peaceful. So beautiful.' Sebalrai shuffled off the heavy furs that had been vital outside and let them drop to the ground. She walked to the brink of the ledge and looked down.

Kell came over and pointed away to the hazy distances. 'See there. Those are the terraces where I worked. I was a ploughboy, and I had control of my own mox . . .' He went on to explain something of his old life: his moving from host family to host family, his lessons at the Tutorium, his long conversations with Gifu . . .

'Which reminds me that we should be about our business.' He gazed on a level into the far distance: the sun was a glowing cloud of deep yellow with a delicate orange corona, but that told him little. He had become attuned to the days and nights and other cycles of the outer world. Was it morning here or close to evening time and the sun's ungathering? He could no longer decide.

Even if the sun goes out, we can still find our way back. Fenrir reminded Kell of a wulf's visual power. And besides, the eye orbs carried lights of their own that could guide them.

It was a long but easy climb down from the heights to the middle terraces. By the time they arrived there the city of Odal was visible through the golden haze; a sweep of crystal and metal curving around the further shores of the Central Lake. Perth's distant ramparts could just be seen as a suggestion of hills reaching up to blend with the shimmering sky.

'You have everything here.' Sebalrai was looking about herself in wonder. 'You would want for nothing.'

'Perhaps that's why I had to leave.' Kell was not being dramatic. He smiled faintly at the spectre of the past. 'If you want for nothing, you strive for nothing.'

'Striving and strife are cruel sisters,' Sebalrai replied as she remembered her own cold upbringing. 'I would have given much for this shelter and safety and peace.'

'Would have? What has changed? You could always stay here?' Kell spoke lightly. He was teasing her, and he failed to notice the shifting light in her eyes. But Skjebne was wise to it, and Fenrir smelled the deep stirring in the girl's blood.

'I have spotted Gifu,' Skjebne said almost at once. It broke the spell of the moment nicely. An eye orb came spinning back and then led the three friends along the grassy track to where the old man was dozing in the sun. Not far off, his mox was to be seen crunching on ripe lantern apples, using the bulk of its body to push a way through the crackle of twigs and underbrush deeper into the grove.

'Ha! He once told me off for letting that happen!' Kell laughed and immediately afterward, as though a gate had opened, felt the sadness and hurt of loss rise up quickly inside him.

'He's waking.' Skjebne withdrew the eye orbs so they were out of the old landsman's sight. But what would he make of the wulf, and of a girl who should not by rights exist in the world?

'Gifu . . . Gifu my heart-father. I'm sorry I startled you.' Kell hunkered down and stroked the old man's grey hair as he struggled from slumber. Gifu roused and rubbed his sleep-reddened eyes and called a command to the mox, who cheerfully ignored him.

'Out! Out of it beast!'

He began to stand, groaning with stiffness.

'He doesn't see you Kell.' Skjebne said, shocked. 'Sebalrai, what are you doing?'

'Nothing – nothing! Kell, I am not using my gift. We stand here plainly in front of his eyes.'

'Then the All Mother has done this to him. Oh, Gifu –' Kell gripped the man by the shoulder and Gifu yelled out in fear and swiped this way and that at his invisible assailant. Kell stumbled away.

Don't frighten him further, Fenrir said. *I can calm him*. And without moving and without any pause the wulf touched the old slow-eye's thoughts and allowed them to settle.

Then he padded up to the man where he sat slumped back against the cushiontree. The wulf sniffed and touched Gifu's face with his nose and stepped lightly into the world of his mind.

He is happy. Gifu thinks it has always been like this. He does not remember the time of darkness you told me about, Kell. He does not remember you either . . . He cannot remember, for the thoughts have been taken from him. He is unsynnig. Untainted. Innocent. Today had no beginning for him and will have no end.

'I shall destroy her,' Kell said with a softness that gave weight to his threat.

She is with us now –

Fenrir took a step back and cocked his head curiously at the change that came over Gifu's face. An awareness appeared.

'You will not destroy me,' Gifu's voice said with a calm assurance. 'Even though I know you can bring the doom down from the sky, in doing so you will wipe out yourself and all of those you love in this place, and all of the innocents who dwell here.'

'I wonder if that troubled me in Thule?' Kell smiled but it came out as a grimace. He forced his hatred of the All Mother to cloak the fears he felt for the safety of his friends.

'If not, then you would be stupid. And I don't think that is the case.'

'Why have you done this to him?' Kell asked, turning the direction of the conversation. It was so strange to be talking to Gifu, yet speaking of him as though he were elsewhere.

'What is going through your soul now, Kell of Perth? What price do you pay for your memories? Would it not be so much better to live your life entirely in this moment, empty of grief, in a perfect now?'

'Like a gyldenfish stuck in a pond! We have had this conversation before,' Kell sneered, but finding it hard to show Gifu such disdain.

She is very afraid. Fenrir slid the revelation into Kell's mind like a subtle blade. *She has many motives for stealing the thoughts of her people . . .*

'You are a hypocrite,' the boy went on and felt a soaring excitement in the contempt he displayed before the source of his childhood terrors. 'I would guess that you keep all of *your* memories close by you, Goddess – sealed in a weorthan core deep beneath the city . . . I know I am right. My blood tells me I am right.'

Before you were born, things were different here Kell. There was a trembling in Fenrir's impressions as he hunted out a truth.

'Without my memories Perth could not continue –' Gifu gave a smile that was not his own.

Kell, she altered the minds of the people because *you had been born! There is more . . . No . . . She is withdrawing . . .*

'Not in the way you want it to.' Kell stood up and took a backward pace away from Gifu who had in an instant become just an old man dozing lightly in the sun.

A change in the quality of the light alerted Kell that the day would soon be ending. Briefly he considered that the Goddess would ungather the sun prematurely as a mean punishment for his trespass. But that was not so. This meeting had been different. This time Kell held all the advantage.

'Goodbye, Gifu, my dear friend.' Tears came and he wiped them away self-consciously. 'If we meet again then you will remember me, and you will know the face of Wierd.'

Kell turned and walked quickly away, leaving Sebalrai and Fenrir to take a last look at the world he had known before they hurried to go with him back to the cleft in the rocks.

Darkness arrived when they were still some way from their destination. It happened very suddenly, as if the All Mother took no pleasure now in the magnificence of the ungathering. At once the eye orbs blazed like beacons, two ahead and two behind and one − Skjebne's point of presence − sailing above the group as they attained the ledge they sought. Far away Kell could see a loose cluster of sky gleams drifting higher even than their present level. He explained them in a brief impression to Fenrir.

And they dare not come closer. His head was filled with glee. *The All Mother will not risk my rage!*

There is more to the matter than you realise, Fenrir told him. They reached the entrance to the tunnel. Kell and Sebalrai put on their furs and tried to imagine how the cold would feel after the enclave's kind warmth.

I don't understand you.

The wulf trotted ahead, reading the air that streamed past him. Right now it still flowed outwards from Perth, but soon the freezing wind from Outside would find them, bringing other possible dangers of its own.

Kell, your birth was a turning point in the Wierd of Perth. I snatched that from the All Mother's mind surely enough. But there are other things, much deeper . . . I saw the true face of the Goddess, Fenrir said prompted by the boy's swift flash of impatience.

And he revealed that face without further hesitation. And in the knowledge Kell felt stronger, even as Shamra's clear image broke his heart.

3

Hugauga

For a time he would say nothing about it, nor would Fenrir betray his loyalty. They returned to *Skymaster* which immediately continued on its journey without any apparent prompting from its occupants. Skjebne wondered if the ship was coming to know the ways of the crew beyond a simple obedience to their commands. Perhaps all of the great orbs were beings in their own right, invested with awareness and an intelligence that helped to shape their purpose. Maybe they too had waited down all the long years until the Ice began to recede, and were ready now to take their place in shaping the future of the world.

Skjebne smiled in nurturing such grand romantic thoughts and deliberately brought his speculation to an end. He was sitting in the crystal room gazing at a snowscape of cloudtops many hundreds of spans below him. They glowed a soft blue-white beneath the earliest traces of dawn. The She-Wulf-Claw-Moon was gone now; it had moved too close to the sun and would not be visible for the next day or so, when it could then be seen low in the evening sky. Skjebne marvelled at the beautiful symmetry of the heavens and briefly wished that Wierd would gift the lives of men with patterns of such predictable elegance.

There was a sudden busy flurrying of wings in the room and Tsep appeared. The little man–bat fluttered around the seamless walls before settling impertinently on Skjebne's knee, then looked up at him with the mischievous not-quite-to-be-trusted grin of an alley urchin.

'If you bite me, I'll squash you.' Skjebne's face was serious and set, though there was some humour in his tone – as much as he dared in his youngling relationship with the hreaomus.

Would I find your blood bitter, gefera?

'Never that.' He let himself relax a little. Tsep licked his thin black lips with a long red tongue.

Then perhaps, when you're asleep . . . He continued before Skjebne could compose a reply. *I have two items of news for you, and who can predict which is to be more significant? The boy Kell has told us what Fenrir told him of the true face of the All Mother – which is to say, he let the thought slip and I caught it as easily as a dusk-moth bewildered by the moon. The other . . .*

Tsep concentrated his mind and Skjebne found his attention distracted, and then drawn to what he was thinking; to the image the other had put in his head.

'More orbs! Many of them – smaller than this room!'

Machines for local travel. I have been exploring the passageways and chambers of the great orb, as you know, and came upon this place a short time ago. It means that the Skymaster *can stay at a safe distance while –*

'Yes yes, I know what it means!' Skjebne framed his intention and the supportive fields around him reconfig-ured themselves and lifted him to a standing position. Outside the ghostly scape of clouds was rising up around them, and seconds later the room was lashed by a silent blizzard of snow.

'Our journey is ending, it seems. Those travel orbs will come in useful, little Tsep.' He chuckled. 'Perhaps there is not so much difference between the moon's way and the lives of men after all, eh?'

The chamber was large, perhaps four or five times the volume of the crystal room. Its walls were constructed in a honeycomb design with cells of different sizes, each cell housing an orb. Most of them were eye orb sized, but half a dozen were larger and contained the travel orbs that Tsep had revealed to Skjebne.

The room hummed with power and the air was filled with its potential. Skjebne recognised the nature of this energy: he exerted his will and the patterns of cells rearranged themselves elegantly, bringing one of the travel orbs closer. Its hatchway folded aside and the dark interior was suddenly illuminated by constellations of tiny lights.

'Have patience, *Skymaster*,' Skjebne announced. 'We'll go when *we* are ready.'

'By the Rad, but this is a puzzle,' Hora said. 'I am confused . . .' Tsep looked as though he was about to make comment on that, but Skjebne silenced him with a glare. 'The entire chamber shifted around us, and yet we moved not a hand's width!'

'I have suspected for some time that the great orb is untroubled by notions of inside or outside, near or far.' Skjebne looked about himself excitedly, nervously. 'I think it moulds its metals to our will, or its own. *How* it does so is a problem for tomorrow.'

'You think we have reached Hugauga now?' Kell wondered.

'What I cannot tell you the *Skymaster* knows for sure. Let's go back to the room of controls to learn more.'

Minutes later they had studied the map of lights but were no closer to answering Kell's question. 'One scape looks much like another when it's made of glowing lines,' Hora grumbled. 'How do we know which is our destination?'

'We don't.' Skjebne eased himself up and faced his companions. 'We must put all of our faith in the orbs. *Skymaster* has borne us away from our own land into the territory of strangers. We have allowed it to do so without complaint. At the very least let it complete its task and see us safe in Hugauga.'

There was nothing of any substance to argue over, since the mission itself had its roots in Kell's vision of Feoh and what her dream-image had told him. But practical things could be done to prepare the best chances for the group. These included leaving Hora and Fenrir aboard *Skymaster* for now: both the wyrda and the wulfen had played a significant part in the destruction of Thule and Helcyrian. If the eyes of the Sustren were active in Hugauga, as Skjebne fully expected them to be, then a scarlet-haired warrior and a lean-limbed wulf would endanger the whole party from the outset.

Hora saw the sense of that and didn't argue. Fenrir was not so accepting.

But I am useless here. Surely Sebalrai could shroud me?

'As long as my attention stayed with you, your body would be invisible to men's eyes,' the girl said. 'But if I was distracted, or hurt . . .'

'We are entering a land of magics if Feoh spoke true,' added Kell. 'None of us knows who would fare best or worst down there. But at least we can take obvious precautions.'

'You would not fare too well in a fight, Skjebne.' Hora looked angry and concerned both together. He hated the thought of two children and an almost-crippled man going into danger by themselves.

'I'll stay in the travel orb close at hand. Kell and Sebalrai will venture into Hugauga with Tsep. I can deploy eye orbs to help watch over them . . . Hora, there is no truly safe way to do this!'

The big warrior tutted and frowned – a clear indication to Skjebne that he had accepted the point. He smiled fondly at his friend. Poor Hora. He had joined the wyrda for adventure and travel and the passion of killing for a cause and had found only waiting and mystery and the substanceless danger of unknown things. But Hora's moment would come, Skjebne mused, as must all men's who seek to put their hands into the clay of life and shape it to their dreams.

'So, let us be ready.'

Very soon the *Skymaster* dropped below the canopy of cloud into a region of craggy hills protected from the worst of the winds by a mountain shield. It was a bleak land of shifting glooms and sudden fitful sparklings of pale sunlight. Steep-sided gulleys carried meltwater in cascading torrents down to the lowlands. Sculptures of sun-moulded ice hung from the crags. At first it appeared to be a desolate region, surely unpopulated; but then an eye orb skimmed the face of a cliff and was confronted by a company of dragons jutting from the rock; perhaps twenty of them formed from a dark grey yet glossy metal. They were all uptilted, with sleek fierce heads pointing halfway

41

to the zenith. Their eyes were shining, but black and impenetrable.

'Is this it?' Kell asked. 'Is this Hugauga?'

Skjebne worked the controls and the orb moved along the cliff in a wide searching sweep.

'Possibly. Yes, quite possibly. *Skymaster* has come to a halt, so presumably we have arrived . . . These are wonderful icons, beautifully made.'

Images of the Draca, the ancient Wyrm, added Fenrir. *Wulfenlore makes mention of this creature. It lies curled around the tangled roots of the world, guarding the treasure hoard of Wierd – of all things yet to be. The Draca is prepared to wait for eternity to see the future safe. But, if it is threatened, it will rise up in all its aspects in fire and light to annihilate its enemies. That is why the Wyrm is also known as a being of the sky, the winged beast of vengeance. Even the Godwulf bows down to it in respect.*

'We had better take care not to anger it, then,' quipped Hora. And the company duly laughed in their apprehension – but Kell was noticing Fenrir closely. The wulf's yellow eyes were bright and focused intently on the dragon carvings in the cliff. It was as though he knew their story, but had never actually seen one before. The sight seemed to exhilarate him.

'If Hugauga is here then it must be hidden below the earth.'

Skjebne made adjustments and the eye orb swung away, streaking along the cliff face in an upsoaring arc that brought it quickly to a ravaged plateau. Here the chopped-up ground was softened by a sparse growth of wiry grass and low-spreading thornbrush interspersed with outcrops of dark rock and more of the dragon carvings, which it seemed had been left untouched by an age of storms.

Skjebne gathered several of the orbs and set them to search in an expanding spiral. Very shortly afterwards his intuition was rewarded.

'There.'

He indicated the screen and the company saw that the orb had come to rest above a pit in the earth. It reminded Kell fleetingly of the entrance to Tsep's home caverns. A probe light revealed a passageway sloping downwards into the ground.

'Just wide enough for a travel orb,' Skjebne said with genuine glee.

'Aye, and how will we know what danger you face when you're down there.' Hora was still deeply unhappy. 'Won't the rock prevent us from communicating?'

'Fenrir and Kell are closely mind-linked, Hora: we have the eye orbs that I can send out from the tunnel: we have the threat of *Skymaster* in the sky above Hugauga – all of which might prove unnecessary, for the people there may be benign. Let us not create calamity out of ignorance.'

'Let us not fail to anticipate danger before we walk the path,' Hora countered irritably. But he knew that Skjebne's mind was set, and so went with the others to the chamber of the orbs to see them on their way.

The travel orb offered the same cramped comfort as the ice wain Kell and his friends had used to escape from Perth. There were seats for a pilot and three passengers, and some stowage for immediate provisions. Niches within the hull could accommodate up to four eye orbs, and Skjebne discovered (by accident or the guiding hand of Wierd) that these communicated with the outside of the ship through a system of self-sealing hatches. The physical controls matched those of *Skymaster* itself, but Skjebne was becoming increasingly artful in the use of his mind, admitting to himself that the spheres felt like his friends, or even like facets of his own personality. But these thoughts he kept close-bound to himself for fear of ridicule.

Sebalrai helped him into the travel orb, and when he was seated took her place beside Kell. Tsep nestled comfortably in his pouch within the boy's tunic.

'We will see you shortly, Hora. Don't drink too much *meodu* before our return!'

Skjebne laughed at his own wit as he turned away, so failed to see Hora's fading smile as he closed the rear hatch and sent the orb on its journey . . .

The chamber of the orbs seemed to swirl around itself in a complex dance of rings. Hora moved not one handspan, and although he was watching closely he failed to spot the magic that caused the orb to vanish. Within an eyeblink he was standing alone in the room.

They entered the shaft and found its walls to be worked to a smooth polish, set at an unchanging angle into the ground and varying not a fingerwidth in diameter as the orb progressed along it at a steady speed. Here and there, picked out by the vessel's brilliant lights, the travellers glimpsed large cavities in the stone: crater-like depressions filled by strange smoothly curved shapes of metal with the same haematite gleam as the dragon icons above.

'Sensing devices perhaps,' Skjebne hazarded, trying to sound knowledgeable. His companions grinned at him in open challenge. 'Well, ornamentation possibly . . .'

They let the moment go by, feeling too excited yet too

nervous for either humour or serious discussion. Snatching wild guesses out of the air when they had no true experience of this place served little purpose but to mire them deeper in their own ignorance. All that could be done of any worth was to wait with patience until their destination became clear.

For a while the tunnel walls passed by in a changeless flow. Then the viewport showed a double fork ahead, the shaft splitting suddenly into four identical paths.

'Shall we send eye orbs out to explore the way?' Kell suggested with a slight edge of panic in his voice. Skjebne looked unsure. 'We need only to make a few wrong decisions to become hopelessly lost. Who knows how extensive this labyrinth of tunnels might be!'

Skjebne made a calming gesture, as much to settle himself as the others.

'Kell, this will sound odd to you perhaps. But I feel that the orb knows where it is going –'

'But it's never been here.'

'No, but I think Hugauga has existed for a long, long time. And I think that the knowledge of its location is built into the mind of the *Skymaster*, whose influence directs these lesser machines.'

'So if we do nothing, we will go the right way?' Sebalrai's question was asked with an innocence that also starkly illuminated the heart of Skjebne's belief. He swallowed hard and resisted the impulse to shrug.

'Exactly. Trusting to the orb now is the same as keeping faith with Wierd itself.'

The division of the tunnels was almost upon them and the time for discussion was over. Quite deliberately, Skjebne took his hands from the controls and let his mind settle. The orb sailed on and unhesitatingly entered the first of the right-hand shafts.

'It's done,' Skjebne said, and with a wicked gleam in his eye he continued to let the travel machine direct its own course. Very soon the shaft opened out and the downward angle shallowed until they were moving along a level, high-roofed passage where more of the depressions were visible, each filled with a form of rounded metal, like frozen quicksilver. Out of curiosity Skjebne deployed an eye orb and sent it skimming over to examine one of the shapes. He and Kell and Sebalrai huddled round a window screen as the eye's observation lights blinked on.

'It is intricately wrought. Look there.' Skjebne indicated a complex tracery of fine lines seemingly etched in the convex surface. 'It seems to be folded around itself . . . If it is a sensor, it hasn't sensed us yet.'

'It looks like a cat deep asleep,' Sebalrai said, though the others were too intent to take much notice.

Impulsively Skjebne guided the eye orb closer, closer, until it touched the surface of the shape. A faint and subtle glow seemed to glimmer through its metal.

'Interesting . . .'

He repeated the act. The orb bounced softly a second time. Again. Again.

And the shape sprang to life, writhing around until it became a trap of talons, a flash of red eyes, a pair of savage jaws that lashed out and crushed down upon the orb and destroyed it in an instant amidst a storm of fiery sparks.

Something spun fast past the forward viewpoint. Skjebne and his friends watched as the orb was hurled across the wide passageway and sent crashing into the far wall. It exploded into a spray of fragments that went scattering far along the tunnel floor.

And all around them now, roused by this initial disturbance, many of the metal forms were stirring; unfolding out from the walls, spreading wings of membranous steel and launching themselves into the gloom. Not slumbering cats, but proud sleek dragons that soared with the elegance of a corvus bird and raked the air with high piercing cries.

'You shouldn't have done that, Skjebne.'

In other circumstances they would have laughed at the inanity of Kell's comment. But the boy's skin was pale and his eyes dark with the same fear that showed on the faces of his friends.

Tsep freed himself from Kell's tunic pouch and fluttered down on to the viewport ledge.

You have alerted them. It is the same with the Hreaomus. Wake one and sleep leaves us all.

'What do we do about it?'

The answer had already been made. As far as the travellers knew, the eye orb was weaponless. It had also been allowed to choose its own way, with the result that Skjebne was uncertain of their return course. Besides which, the warriors of the Draca were surrounding the orb so there could be no escape.

And now another of the monsters, ten times larger than the rest, rose up from a pit in the passageway floor and came streaking and screaming towards them.

The huge impact that Skjebne expected never arrived. He thought he might have lived to see the creature's huge claws slice through the fabric of the orb, before he died in a terrible glory of fire and metal and blood. There was a sudden sideways movement, as though the beast had nudged the orb or tried to grab it in its talons. But then the dragon withdrew: the travellers watched its sleek body stream past; it was gone, reappearing a moment later some distance away, hooking itself to the ceiling. It had a long lizard shape, an elegant flexible neck, a graceful tail that ended in a single fearsome barb, and large bat-like wings tipped with blades. It looked back at the troublesome orb with fierce intelligent eyes.

'It could have smashed us easily,' Skjebne said in a whisper, 'but it did not . . .' Patterns of lights began flowing across the panel of controls and Kell started as though he had been snatched from a reverie.

'Oh, Fenrir is contacting me . . . Wait . . . Wait. There is so much to understand . . .'

The others watched the boy's eyes grow distant as he listened to the wulf's silent communication. He frowned several times, but nodded also as his comprehension grew. Meanwhile, the travel orb hung stationary in the tunnel deep underground, and the swarming draca attached themselves once more to the walls. The moment of crisis had passed, though not the probability of danger.

'What are you learning, boy?' Skjebne asked, snappish as his fear subsided. Kell made a sign to be patient, as though he was a Tutor of Perth, precious in his knowledge, not wanting interruption while he reflected upon profound things. Skjebne tutted and sighed, folded his arms and glared at Sebalrai for her sympathy. She kept a neutral expression and resisted the impulse to smile.

'The Wyrm knew we were coming,' Kell said presently, almost woodenly, as though he was passing on these ideas without either believing or disbelieving them. 'Or, that is to say, the Thrall Makers suspected our arrival – eventually, as part of the pattern of things. The Draca . . . Fenrir was right and not right . . . The Draca exists but as a force, a guardian force . . .'

'Is it Wierd then?'

'Nothing is Wierd.' Kell was speaking the wulf's thoughts directly now. 'But Wierd is everything. We all have a part to play in its weave –'

'This much is already apparent.'

'All of the threads go back a long time. The Ice has burdened the land for thousands of seasons, but the roots of Wierd go down deeper than that. Mankind was already trying to – to *change the patterns*, even when the world was warm, before the great Wintering began . . .'

Kell's eyes refocused and he looked at his friends rather sheepishly. 'Fenrir does not really understand the thoughts that are in his own head. They are too big and too complicated to know all at once.'

'There is enough to unravel them,' Skjebne said with unexpected sympathy. He again felt the sense of significance that had first come to him as Kano led them from Perth; as he and his friends had looked across the hidden valley of the orbs; as the last dark hours of Thule had unfolded. Once more he knew that wheels were turning within wheels – men had set them in motion, but all were caught up now in their inevitable dance.

'So are the Thrall Makers here in Hugauga?'

'Fenrir says no. By and large they are very distant . . . Some have disappeared into obscurity, hidden in the flesh and in the mind.' Kell smirked. 'That doesn't make sense.'

'It doesn't matter for now. What of the Thrall Maker Wrynn?'

'He's here! Suddenly the boy's face was alight with anticipation. He looked beyond his companions and out into the tunnel.

And there was a red-robed man with a face as sharp as a *seax* blade, standing right beneath the fearsome form of the huge metal dragon.

The walls were at least as alive as the beast. That was Kell's first and overriding impression as they stepped down from the travel orb. The rock was tinged with a patina of silvery grey – the same substance perhaps from which the Draca was formed. It smelled strongly of hot iron and lightnings, and seemed somehow to be *busy* underneath the threshold of Kell's full awareness. There was a knowingness to the cave which the travellers found to be both comforting and deeply disturbing. The place was a presence here as much as they were.

The younglings supported Skjebne as he walked stiffly towards the man named Wrynn, who watched him approach dispassionately. Kell's gaze kept straying to the vast creature above him, but the monster was quiescent, curled about itself although doubtless fully alert. Tsep rode defiantly upon the boy's shoulder and kept up a constant chitter-chatter of thoughts and impressions that Kell only half noticed, his attention being fixed on the imposing figure of the Thrall Maker.

'So, you have reached me at last.'

The arrivals registered the words a moment after they were said. To Kell they did not seem like words at all, nor exactly thoughts. Just the lightest touch upon his consciousness. Had the man's mouth moved? Had the Draca spoken? Was the cave itself enfolding them in its unfathomable mind? Tsep was of no help at all and this was much too difficult to untangle.

'Sir.' Skjebne made an awkward bow then looked Wrynn frankly in the face. 'If you were expecting us, then I take it you know who we are?'

'I know something of you, though I know more about the parts you have been chosen to play. Your existence has long been predicted: I came to hear of your names only when the Seetus made that information clear to me.'

'You have met the Seetus?' Kell was startled and pleased and possibly a little envious all at the same time.

'Met is not quite accurate. I have never stood before him, as you did Kell. He is a unique being, the child of our tears, and he shows himself in the flesh only rarely. The fact that he rose from the sea not just through the bidding of the Shore Folk, but because you were there, is testament to your importance. You are the yeast that ferments the beer, as loyal Hora might say.'

It was humour of a sort, Kell supposed; Wrynn's attempt to make them feel more at their ease. The Thrall Maker smiled faintly at his own imagery and his mouth seemed very dark inside.

He went on. 'However, you have travelled some distance to speak with me and we should do that in comfort. Hugauga is extensive, spreading far beneath the ground, but I have chambers nearby. Come along now, and your curiosity shall be answered.'

Wrynn turned and beckoned them on. And his hand was as grey and metallic as the walls and the floor and the massive body of the Wyrm.

51

4

Wrynn's Tale

They walked but a short way, though travelled a great distance through the passages of Hugauga – the maze town, a place that had no centre and no edge. Skjebne understood that invisible fields existed here, as they did within *Skymaster* and the other great orbs; forces sensitive to a man's will but not compliant to it, allowing great accomplishments with the ease and rapidity of a thought. Certainly this place was ancient and complex, built by an unknown culture that seemed to have vanished by now. And yet it possessed an *onweardnes* of its own, a spirit that was both alien and cold and quite likely powerful beyond words.

Skjebne mentioned none of this to his companions. The younglings walked beside him absorbed in the wonder of the place (though Sebalrai was very nervous and kept fading in and out of his sight). Tsep clung to Kell's shoulder and chittered constantly with excitement, occasionally making an astute observation that the boy barely heard.

And at the head of the party strode Wrynn, tall and upright in his confidence of Hugauga; sombre of face with the weight of recent events. He led and the others followed in silence. And once Skjebne glanced upward to see if the great dragon accompanied them . . . And perhaps it did, for there was a rippling in the metallic surface of the cave ceiling which sometimes suggested the claws and wings and huge pointed head of the beast.

Before long they emerged into a spacious cavern, the floor of which formed a border around a translucent pool whose waters were a breathtaking shade of blue green. Illuminations rising from the depths cast the mystical light around the cavern walls. These were latticed with steps carved in the rock, many of the flights tilted and hung at impossible angles. Each led to the doorway of a dwelling, or else to a further passage that vanished quickly into its own gloom. And again Skjebne sensed the unseen influence that had helped him walk so far along the tunnel, such that his injured leg had been no encumbrance at all.

'Is this the heart of Hugauga?' Kell ventured to ask. Wrynn turned and smiled, surprising his guests by the silvery dark gleam of his teeth.

'Anywhere here is the heart of Hugauga. But, to answer you plainly, we are nowhere near its centre. My chambers are just a little way on.' He pointed. 'There.'

They looked and Sebalrai's mouth stayed open and Kell laughed uneasily, for the entrance to the Thrall Maker's home was directly above them, to be reached by an elegant arc of steps that began quite normally, then curved up and round to the vertical. And even as they watched, a man from a neighbouring dwelling appeared on the ceiling and waved down to them before proceeding to cross the cavern roof with the ease and assurance of a fly.

'Hugauga is a law unto itself,' Wrynn said mischievously. Then his smile faded as he thought of other things. 'Which is why it has survived for so long.'

Without preamble he mounted the steps and his guests followed and were only briefly afraid. The ground they had walked upon tilted and took on the appearance of a wall that dropped slowly away until it was the ceiling, and the entrance to Wrynn's apartments stood naturally before them.

They entered at his invitation and found themselves in comfortable quarters, in a bubble of warmth in the rock; low ceilinged, warm and cosy and illuminated by a few soft globes of reddish-yellow light, self-supported in the air. Skjebne asked if it was ligetu light, with which he was familiar. But Wrynn called it plasma and said it was held in place by the soul of the house that attended to his every need.

He disappeared briefly to another room while his guests settled themselves down on to cushions, and returned soon after accompanied by a broad silver platter laden with food. The platter floated beside him, and without instruction lowered itself to a convenient height between the visitors as the Thrall Maker started his tale.

'Long ago the Earth changed beyond Man's capacity to prevent it, and the Ice began to spread from the poles and encroach upon the body of the globe. Perhaps this occurrence was part of the natural web of cycles of the planet and the space in which it is embedded. Or maybe it was only a byproduct of humanity's growth. This is past anyone's power to know. But it was clear that the whole world would be engulfed in time, and that the Wintering would last for many hard long desperate generations.

'Fear grew. It tore at the heart of all peoples. But there

was determination too, that the oncoming disaster would not wipe Mankind from the memory of the world. Huge endeavours were started, vast enterprises in the name of survival which spanned continents and cultures and their tiny, petty differences, and the lifetimes of individual women and men.

'A fleet of orbs was built. You are familiar with some of them – *Skymaster* and *Windhover* and the others you know. These few are the ones that remained. No one knows why; possibly as a means of allowing the sons and daughters of the Ice to follow the Sigel Rad opened up so long before by the original sailors to the stars. But it has never happened, partly because the well-meaning Wyrda Craeftum retained the knowledge of the Rad without truly understanding it. Such is the nature of simply remembering facts, rather than exploring ideas.

'Even so, the orbs have their part to play now. You have already discovered that the Universal Wheel guides them at least as much as they are governed by the wishes of men. And the Wheel, it must be said, embodies mysteries that neither you nor I nor the wyrda may ever understand, but which connect us all at a fundamental level . . .'

(And here Wrynn paused briefly to look around himself and then at the leaden pallor of his right hand before continuing).

'Ages ago the orbs swarmed upwards into the skies and vanished forever from sight. And that must have been a magnificent spectacle to witness. But whatever other feelings were held deep inside the people who remained, their overriding passion was to outlast the ravages of the Ice.

'You may know that a body is composed of millions

55

upon millions of cells. Each of us is a true community. Within each cell there are threads, and upon the threads are the jewels of command that shape our intimate being. Let it be said here and now that those commands are directed by Wierd, which exists above and beyond them all. The cosmos itself is a wonderful tapestry of threads and jewels, but Wierd outspans it easily. Everything that exists is just a single fleeting spark of thought in the omnipresent mind of Wierd.

'Well, it came about that the ancient mystics found a way of teasing out the threads of life and reconfiguring the jewels upon them. Living things could be reviewed and reformed to endure the cold more successfully. I know you are friends with the wulfen pack, Kell. Ages ago the storm wulves were the product of the mystics' experiments, created anew and restitched into the weave of the land. But then, how interesting it is that a gem may be turned and endlessly examined, its every facet known and under-stood – only for a stray gleam of sunlight to pass through it and cast a different and wonderfully unexpected colour. The wulfen did more than survive; they changed of their own accord and developed the synerthic abilities that you have come to know and rely upon. This was indeed a surprising and valuable treasure, for it allowed human beings to be similarly altered to speak mind-to-mind without the encumbrance of words. On rare occasions a child is born who quite naturally exhibits these powers. More usually the gift is cultivated by one or more artificial means, as it was with your dear friend Feoh – though I shall speak of her later.

'Aside from all of this, because the work was unpredict-able while the march of the Ice was relentless, the preglacial peoples did whatever else they could to prepare. The enclaves were carved out of the ground. Some made use of the land's natural features, while others were created through the sheer force of the industrial arts. And people clad themselves in exotic armour, became shackled to it inside and out. The drengs of Helcyrian evolved as one product of this dark work.

'Imagine the thrill and the terror and the fire of determination that must have existed during that time. Never before or since has humanity reached such a peak of achievement. They were fine and noble centuries, for the most part. And as the blizzards lashed the lands and the oceans alike, and as the world grew as white and crystalline as a pebble of sea-washed quartz, men and women in their millions went underground to outlast the greatest hard-long-dark of them all.

'To begin with they were as one people. All across the globe the communities enjoyed a free exchange of ideas, linked as they were by the mind of a device that the legends know by the name of Little Sister. She was a presence embodied in crystal and in other substances, the soul of a machine that wrapped the world around in an elegant web of filaments – Although once, at the start, she was human; but again I will explain that idea in its proper order.

'Little Sister was both symbol and saviour to the communities that lived below the earth, adrift in their dream of a future they might never live to see. And as time went by and as generations appeared and grew and faded again like flowers, so the links of communication were broken between the enclaves and, it is said, the heart of Little Sister itself was fractured and tainted, perhaps by terror or loneliness or the lack of human love.

'However it may have been, her original purpose became corrupted and she regretted her great and ancient sacrifice. Lost in the void of her own endless being, she brooded and planned and dreamed of a time when she might live again in the flesh and feel the warmth of the generous sun on her skin. So say many of the root-legends of my people, and events have borne them out.

'To begin with, Little Sister used what limited means she possessed to found a new sect called the Sustren, a sisterhood supple to her will. These women were gifted with many special abilities, some of them conferred through the blood – for Little Sister cultivates her children very carefully – and others through the arts of metal and glass, of which you have bitter, though useful, experience. The Sustren exist to serve two linked purposes, each forged to realise Little Sister's ultimate dream. One, the Sustren learn and master whatever crafts help their Goddess to maintain power over her peoples and bring her closer to her goals. Two, they watch over the newborn in search of a girlchild who will not only remind Little Sister of the way she had been, but who will allow the Goddess to re-embody herself in the world. And that girl has the appearance of –'

'Shamra.'

Kell spoke the word like an agony, like a part of his flesh torn away. As Wrynn had unfolded his tale, and as Kell had seen its direction, he knew he could not keep the terrible secret inside himself any longer. Skjebne looked knowingly into the Thrall Maker's eyes, and Sebalrai put her arm around Kell's shoulder to comfort him, for whatever might happen between the two of them, Kell and Shamra were still heartbonded until one or both decided otherwise.

'That is why she was taken at the village of the Shore People,' Wrynn explained. 'It was Little Sister's first opportunity to spirit Shamra away after she had escaped with you from Perth. The one you call the All Mother had been watching over Shamra very closely since the days of her infancy – And how significant it is, I feel, that the girl should be born at the same time that you were, Kell. This surely proves the guiding hand of Wierd was at work!'

'Little Sister saw herself in Shamra and craved the vessel of her flesh. For centuries that mirror likeness has haunted the ghost in the machine: when children were born whose features resembled the All Mother's original face, she would nurture them as her own and endeavour to possess them in any way that she could – except for the final, ultimate way which has always been beyond her. Until, perhaps now.'

'Explain yourself, mage,' Skjebne said. 'Do you mean that the spirit of Little Sister has found a way to inhabit Shamra's body?'

'She may have. Or she may not,' Wrynn replied without intending to be provocative. He poured himself some refreshment and the silver platter floated to each of his guests in turn so that they could help themselves.

'The matter is a complicated one which pivots on the All Mother's central dilemma. As she is and has been, she is immortal. She has brooded over her children for a span of time beyond imagining, guiding the people along their way according to her will. But what a torment it must have been to watch over that ceaseless parade of human life and to have been detached from it entirely. Little Sister was shackled to her purpose for a bleak and bloodless eternity.

'But then things started to change. The monstrous cold began to abate and the iron grip of the Ice relaxed. By accident, or more likely by the subtle promptings of fate, men and women dreamed of the world beyond their enclaves, and turned their dreams into actions and struggled up to the surface of the earth. Sometimes these emergings were disastrous. My people have heard tell of entire populations wiped out by the creatures that learned to survive on the ice sheets. But other groups were luckier and flourished.

'So it was that Little Sister watched her children leaving; her single, final, fundamental reason for existence was about to be broken. What would be left but an emptiness too terrible to bear. And although I cannot forgive the Goddess for her actions, I can understand them truly, for I think I would have done just the same.

'Little Sister increased her control over the enclaves that remained intact. She composed the Knowledge to create a picture of the world still ice-locked and uninhabitable, filled with terrors. She punished severely the people that persisted in thinking otherwise. Meanwhile, she wielded her influence as best she could on those communities who had reached the surface, but who still relied on the enclave for shelter and protection – Thule being one such domain.'

'Why didn't the All Mother just destroy me?' Kell wanted to know. 'Or, for that matter, why didn't she wipe out Kano and Skjebne and the others before I ever met them?'

'Ah, there you have hit on something that I have long pondered without reaching any definite conclusion. Perhaps instinctively Little Sister knew of your importance:

the cycles of the blood are beyond her control and she could not have predicted Shamra's birth, nor that of Kell the Questioner. But she knew that your lives would be intertwined and was loath to interfere with the powerful reckonings of Wierd. Then again, it might be that your survival *is part of the All Mother's plan,* which may be of a depth and complexity too great for me to fathom.

'However it is, undeniably we sit together now so that I can enlighten you with as much as I know and burden you with as much as I can guess . . .

'If Little Sister ever succeeded in reincarnating herself through Shamra, she would survive only for a human span and then pass away into chaos, that vast ocean of potential from which all created things arise, and to which they return when their time is done. She has become used to existence, in however alien a form. The prospect of not-being is terrifying to her. She cannot contemplate it. She must exist throughout time, but as blood and bone, in womanhood, with a heart that beats. And to that end, she sent the Sustren to seek out my own kind, the Thrall Makers.'

'Now,' Wrynn said, smiling kindly on his guests, 'there is much that I ask you to take on faith, and more that I cannot reveal to you at all. These are dangerous times, critical times, when the great balances of fate could tip either way. A word carelessly spoken might hand the Goddess her ultimate victory. And so I must tread a cautious path and let my heart guide my thoughts . . .

'I have mentioned to you already that the fabric of existence has its arrangement of stitches and threads. The jewelled filaments which instruct the forms of life follow the patterns of that greater tapestry. During their long

61

seclusion under the earth, my kin learned the ways of the weave – and discovered also that they are sensitive to the influence of conscious thought and intention. The Over-mind that is Wierd itself makes use of this sáme process, though on an incomprehensibly larger scale –'

'So, you are saying –'

'I am saying, Skjebne, that my kind have learned the ways of morphological prayer – By touching the soul we can affect the form of things. The Seetus knows this power too; he is himself an outcome of its use. And he in turn has used it to draw the Shore Folk down to the sea and a future in safety.

'Let it be very clear to you now that no Thrall Maker would ever use his gift wantonly. Indeed, no single mage is capable of significant action. We work together to a common aim through the rites of *Gebedraedan* to achieve our ends, in the place of our origin which is called Kairos, the city out of time. There the *drycraeftig*, the magically skilled, arrange the circumstances of the Thrall. For the most part, like children dabbling their feet in the safe shallow waters of the ocean shore, we have slowly accumulated our expertise. It has not been part of our quest to interfere with Wierd's intentions, but rather to understand them more deeply. How can a human mind dare to trespass, to emulate the way of the first great Creative Force?'

'But the All Mother has dared,' Skjebne said before Wrynn had a chance to do so. He had seen the shift of light in the Thrall Maker's eyes and knew that the mage had not wanted to tell them the worst. Now, with the secret spoken and its horror known, the tension shifted and Wrynn settled back a little in his seat.

'Ten seasons ago the Sustren came into Kairos. A trail of rumour and hearsay had led them to our gates. They brought drengs – or creatures like drengs – for their own protection and to intimidate us. But their deeper power lay in the seduction of some of our men-kin and the corruption of their hearts with false promises – Not that their own abilities are false or in any way inadequate. The Sustren have developed their intermental skills to an astonishing degree. They can communicate mind-to-mind over large distances and, to some extent, mimic the synerthic onemindedness of the wulfen and the Shore Folk to act as a single individual. Other members of the sister-hood, like Feoh, are brilliant medical intuitives; women capable of reading the body's map of life energies and freeing blocks to well being . . . Or stopping the flow entirely so that death will quickly follow. I have seen that same gift used to gain understanding of devices and machines, whose grosser forces nevertheless are patterned and planned.

'And above all, these beautiful, dangerous, mysterious creatures are directed by the Goddess, their little sister whose one last ultimate wish is to be like them. And be in no doubt that any *gegilda* of the Sustren will give up her own life to further that aim.

'Unless, of course,' Wrynn added, 'she is Sustren only in name and stays true to a different path. As Feoh does.'

The Makers of the Thrall are drawn from all quarters of the planet. They are born to it, though any one man (and such mages are invariably male) may not recognise his calling until his next life, or his next. A single existence might seem mundane and quite purposeless, but the learning happens anyway and the innocent one is set on his path. All of them, across all times and places, are *gebrooor*, true brothers at the very centre of their hearts.

Wrynn as a child was lucky enough to understand his gift and had come to Kairos – been attracted by careful circumstance to that secluded place – when he was barely older than Kell the Sith was now. Further training led him swiftly and surely through his novitiate, so that by the time of his manhood he was easy in the ways of the illusion glass (that Kell and his companions called weorthan), and had absorbed great quantities of its learning. He could also sing the silent noteless melodies of the *Gebedraedan*; the chants and venerations that tapped into the essence of the forms of life and could alter them, as an emotion artfully evoked might affect the appearance of a human face.

Wrynn the mage, bloodkin of the *drycraeftig*, attained mastery of the most terrifying of the mortal arts and learned its fundamental lesson – that such knowledge would, in its application, confirm and sustain Man's essential humanity, or destroy it utterly and forever.

The Thrall Makers had traced their ancestry back before the Ice and knew that the earliest of their kind had succeeded in transforming the physical structure of life by physical means. They created the wulfen to thrive in the deepest cold, together with a variety of other species including the Aurok and the humble mox, the Hreaomus and the corvus flocks that give meaning to the skies.

Generations later, when the Ice had locked the world around and humanity lay curled like the fragile mouse in its nest beneath the earth, the Brothers of the Thrall succeeded in changing life at a deeper level still, through the very fields of energy which are like the streams that feed the awesome River of Being and send it coursing on towards the brink of time. They came to realise that the instructions held inside living cells are simply the gates that open and close to let these life energies through. The builders of breeds had been tinkering with machinery on a small scale, whereas the Thrall Makers knew how to drive the great engine itself.

By the time of the Thaw, Wrynn's kind had learned that not just life was underpinned by its particular matrix of forces. All created things have their template, and this is no physical thing but a *potential* lying deeper than metal or glass or flesh or bone. And any potential might lie latent or be expressed; a seed or a flower in Wierd's eye.

By this insight, the Thrall Makers achieved some remarkable things. One result of their endeavours was the elegant use of the fields that enshrouded Hugauga and similar strongholds to preserve them all through the years. They also developed what came to be called Radiant Iron, the metal that–did–not–quite–exist, out of which the fearsome Draca was created. Wherever a mage might travel, he took some iron with him that could take the form of a knife or a coin, or a web around his heart or the steely glint in his eye. Thus he was never alone or defence-less. Although, while accepting he was never alone, Wrynn came to see that loneliness could torment the largest multitudes and an empty heart always defeated the fullest of minds.

By the time the Sustren arrived on the streets of Kairos, many of the Thrall Makers knew that times were changing and that the future was outpacing their plans.

The women of the sisterhood were articulate and intelli-gent, deferential yet independent. They were all keenly interested in the lessons the mages had learned, and traded knowledge for knowledge in sharing the secrets of their own esoteric arts. Their skill was thus both practical and profound, though Wrynn and a few others who were clearer-sighted recognised their other darker agenda.

Despite Wrynn's growing apprehension, one among the Sustren delegation caught his eye. This was Feoh, quite newly initiated it seemed, but less gushingly friendly than her sisters – nor quite as deferential in her supplications to the Goddess.

It so happened, by Wierd's playful ways or Feoh's deliberate intention, that she was attracted to Wrynn as well. After meeting almost by chance, Feoh expressed interest in the mage's particular researches and visited his apartments and asked many minute and perceptive questions. The woman displayed a remarkable understanding, not only of the detail of the Thrall Maker's answers, but of the man himself. She read his loneliness as though it were the page of an opened book. And Wrynn knew that she knew. He dreaded the closeness of that insight as much as he dreaded his growing suspicions of the Sustren's deeper aims. But a woman's ephemeral smile has always overpowered a man's unwavering determination, and it was not long before he had risked his life and the fury of his kind by explaining what he feared.

Feoh's response was to speak with him softly through the private hours of the night. She told him of Perth and of Kano's grand plan, of Kell and her other friends; of the adventures they'd had and her mission to find Shamra who had been captured by the dreng-like slayers of the Goddess; the *Slean* that were not truly alive, but were like shadow souls lodged in the alien substance their bodies had become.

When all the words were spoken, Feoh proved her truth with an intimacy that Wrynn had never known before. There was no bribery or deceit in her act. There was only the longing of two hearts cast up on a cold shore who needed once again to know why they were alive.

'Perhaps you think me naïve,' Wrynn said as the telling drew towards its close. 'Maybe young Sebalrai here understands the female wiles and has used them already in a most subtle sorcery . . .' The Thrall Maker smiled yet he seemed to be gazing far away and took no notice of his guests' reaction. 'And Kell, Skjebne – possibly you feel I am like a child for making my promises in the brilliance of passion rather than in cool reflection, after first weighing all possible consequences.'

'Consequences,' said Skjebne, 'of what?'

'Of putting Feoh at risk by abetting her betrayal of the Sustren. Clearly they are corrupting my kind in the name of their Goddess – As I might have been beguiled by Feoh if I am as foolish as I suspect!'

'She would never hurt you.' Kell said this with such a quiet sincerity that the mage was forced to regard him in all seriousness, acquiescing finally with a small bow of his head. 'She tore half her face away to be rid of the All Mother's enchantment. Neither did she think about her own safety when she set off after Shamra. I have never met anybody nobler or more thoughtful of others.'

'I suppose I have been so bound to the ways of my kind that seeing the Thrall Makers tainted has shaken me to the core. But the Sustren's intentions were plain, given Feoh's clear sightedness. Ironically I had suspected her too, and I'm sorry for that now.'

'And yet you still came to Hugauga to meet with us.' Skjebne smiled. 'And you still trusted Feoh's friends enough to tell us this much.'

And the mage too let his mood lighten and was done with his doubts with a brief shrug of his shoulders.

'Feoh thinks that the Sustren women will take some of the Thrall Brothers away from Kairos to the place where the Goddess resides – which is to say, where the soul and essence of the All Mother lies entombed. Nobody knows where in the world it may be, except that in dreams it is known as Arcanum, that hides among the deepest roots of the world.'

'So Feoh now is in Kairos –'

Wrynn nodded. 'And Shamra is imprisoned at Arcanum. We have need to take the greatest care, for if Little Sister discovers our plans she will do all that she can to destroy us.'

'So . . .' Kell did not know whether to ask this as a question. 'You will guide us back to Kairos and take us to Feoh.'

'That much I can do.'

'And in return?' Skjebne said.

'I know that Feoh will want to stay with you as you journey on to Arcanum. I cannot leave her now, for I love her and I think that her feelings for me are as sure. Let me come with you, and I will offer what help and protection I can.'

'Once again,' said Kell, 'we have to choose between the stealth of a few or the strength of many. Should we try to take Arcanum by storm? We have the wulfen pack and the men of the wyrda –'

'Our assault begins with skilful protections.'

So saying, and before the others could react to stop him, the Thrall Maker rubbed his hands together and offered them out, and blew a grey dust at their eyes.

5

Children Of The Wyrm

Tsep shrieked and tried to flitter away from the billowing cloud. But it engulfed him as effectively as it wreathed around Skjebne and Sebalrai and Kell, who struggled, choking, out of their seats and tried to stagger away.

For one dreadful second Kell watched Sebalrai's flesh turn grey. He lifted his hand in a futile attempt to defend her – and drew back horrified to see that the same thing was happening to him. Skjebne also, flailing about as though attacked by a swarm of bees, was darkening like a shadow of himself; though all of this was fleeting and seemed over with swiftly. The smoky powder sank into the pores of the skin and was drawn down under it, so that within a very few seconds Kell's colour returned to normal and he was able to grab Sebalrai and hold her close as her own trembling abated.

Skjebne was outraged and spluttered some half-articulate demand for explanation. And by way of reply Wrynn produced a knife from his robes and slashed at the other man's hand. The blade cut cleanly and the skin and the flesh opened up.

'No!' Kell shoved Sebalrai away and reached for his own weapon, a shorter stabbing dagger. Meanwhile Tsep reoriented himself and clawed at the Thrall Maker's face and eyes.

'Get away – get away! You don't understand my purpose. Be still!' Wrynn made some brief hand passes and the fields of influence that had allowed the group to recline in the air, and which supported the floating food platter, now formed a cushion around Tsep and moved him gently aside. Similarly Kell felt his weaponed hand taken by an invisible grip, which forced it downwards and to his side.

As for Skjebne, after his initial shock he stood and watched with a growing amazement as the blood on his palm vanished like vapour, and the flesh closed of its own accord, and the skin formed over the trace of the wound and a moment later was whole and unblemished again.

'Now that,' he was forced to admit, his voice shaking slightly, 'was impressive.'

Nearby Kell steadied his nerves and so as not to provoke the mage further, slid his dagger back into its belt thong and moved half in front of Sebalrai to shield her.

'The Radiant Iron takes many forms and has an even greater range of uses.' Wrynn held up his own arms now so that the loose sleeves slid back to show the grey pallor of his skin. 'You will come to know its ways. I am not troubled much by appearances, so I am not sensitive to the colour of the metal. If you are, then you can keep the iron in abeyance deep in your bones, until such time as it may serve you.'

'It makes you whole again!'

The mage laughed. 'Ah, only abstemious living can do that. The Radiant Iron will preserve and repair you up to a point. Too severe an injury will overwhelm its capacity to mend . . . Now, let me apologise. I shocked you, whereas my intention was to bestow on you a gift as a token of our friendship. The metal also links you with the Draca; and although its forms may not follow your wishes or instructions, the children of the Wyrm will be sensitive to your needs.'

Wrynn looked upon them for a moment longer, as though assessing how the amalgam had melded with their blood. He gave a brisk nod.

'Now I think we must make our final preparations to leave. I did not presume to decide on the outcome of our meeting, so I have not packed all that I will need. Also, I must speak with some of the inhabitants of Hugauga, friends of the Thrall Brothers who look after this outpost and work hard to further our knowledge of the Draca and the substance of which it is made.'

'As for us,' Skjebne glanced over at Kell, 'we will let our friends aboard the orb know what has happened. They will be wondering . . .'

His voice faltered and he looked at the boy's face in concern. Kell was frowning intently, while at his shoulder Tsep's agitation was plain.

'What's troubling him?' Wrynn asked.

'I don't know – Kell?'

'I can't hear Fenrir in my mind. I don't feel him anywhere nearby . . .' He faced his friends and his eyes were bleak.

'I don't know what's happened, or how. But I think that *Skymaster* has gone.'

Wrynn took them quickly back along the passageways of Hugauga until they came to the place where the travel orb had waited. There was room enough for all inside; and despite the seriousness of the situation, Wrynn couldn't help but admire and be curious about the workings of the machine; and Skjebne couldn't help but be pleased to explain them to him.

The orb soared swiftly through the tunnels, accompanied a short distance behind by the monstrous dragon that had greeted the newcomers upon their arrival. As they went, so the passengers noticed that the walls streaming past were flickering with waves of motion that formed brief patterns and sigils on the stone. And they were amazed to see that the skin of the Thrall Maker's arms *was mirroring these messages*, rippling as though in sympathy with the larger agitation.

'There has been a disturbance above,' Wrynn said. And this was no sooner spoken than the travel orb emerged from the ground and soared in a wide upcurving track above the desolate scape. Nearby an outcrop of grey rocks folded aside and the dragon burst out and flew free, rising on strong dark wings through the grey-black overcast of storm clouds – but not entirely black, for somewhere beyond them a huge light was moving; or maybe many lights that cast strange flashes and glimmerings across the cliffs and canyons of cloud.

'This is something I have not seen before,' Wrynn told his companions. 'Nor has the Draca witnessed such a phenomenon.'

'Is it natural?'

'*Skymaster* would not run from thunder and lightning, Kell,' Skjebne said. 'Is there still an absence?'

Kell's eyes shifted and he noticed his own mind and, a moment later, his shoulders slumped.

'No sign. The orb has gone.'

73

'It can't have been destroyed. There would be traces on the ground . . . Fire . . .' Sebalrai's attempt to comfort was little help, though her point was well made. Skjebne seated himself at the travel orb's controls and set the vehicle to follow a sweeping path that searched the ground thoroughly around the entrance to Hugauga.

Meanwhile, high above, Wrynn's dragon rose past the cloud canopy that was lit with reds and golds by the sun's low-angled light. The dome of the sky was littered with glistening splinters, it saw: and it wheeled round just in time to see the nearest one bearing down upon it.

Wrynn jolted as though he'd been struck and staggered back, briefly dazed.

'The light! The Draca is attacked!'

He had no time for more. Whatever had pounced on the dragon was now dropping swiftly through the clouds – brilliant sparks, many of them, shattering apart like sundered gemstones. A few streaked away and were lost among the hills; some swung low to the ground and raced across the scrub; several moved purposefully towards the dragon icons jutting from the cliff; and one launched itself directly at the travel orb and its startled occupants.

Skjebne hauled the control stick sideways and the orb responded instantly, rolling aside as the light flashed past. Some kind of crackling energy rocked the craft and tumbled it almost to the ground.

'This is the work of the Sustren,' Wrynn declared. He had been standing at the window portal, and now needed to take tight hold to save himself from falling. 'Somehow they have found the way to Hugauga.' He saw the look on Kell's face and read his concern. 'Do not worry about the people here, for the place is well protected. Let us look to our own safety now.'

No sooner had he spoken than two things happened at once to prove the worth of his words.

Out of the sky fell the dragon, not in defeat but with an attack ship clasped in its talons. The vehicle was lens-shaped and sleek, its metal flowing elegantly with colour; jade and lapis, amber and deep garnet red. Perhaps it was signalling danger or defeat . . .

And across the broad face of the cliffs the icons of the Draca burst into fiery life. Flames and meteors and particles of light erupted from their jaws and flashed into the sky. One early lucky shot hit another of the craft as soon as it appeared, wreathing it in rainbows and then exploding it apart. Another, badly winged, followed a wavering track that took it below the brink of the plateau: it left a trail of sparks and smoke, and then was swiftly destroyed when it came within range of the guardians of the bluff.

But whoever piloted the ships were either foolhardy or completely dedicated to their task. The attackers came on, more and more of them swarming above the hills. Wrynn's dragon, having rent its prey asunder, swooped round and struck another from the sky with the power of its wings – which it then folded to drop with the elegance of a blade into the path of yet another vehicle.

'It will be relentless in its defence of the settlement.' Wrynn eased himself away from the portal. 'And the people of Hugauga can hide deep inside the earth until the danger is over or the enemy are stopped. But we must look to protect ourselves. Does this orb have weapons?'

'None that I have found yet,' Skjebne admitted.

'And its parent craft, the *Skymaster*, has vanished. So, I think we should return below ground.'

Skjebne needed no further prompting. The entrance to Hugauga was not far away, and he kept the orb low – level with the scrubtops – until the aperture appeared. In the heavens above a battle was raging: the huge dragon plucked ships from the air and either crushed them or tore them to pieces. And its body shone with power and its wings were made of flame. Further off yet no less effective, the guardians spat their missiles and washed the cliffs with waves of flickering white incandescence as the attack ships came on and came on in a seemingly endless profusion.

But Skjebne and his friends turned their backs on all of this. Without hesitation he sent the orb plunging downwards into the tunnels. And this time the journey was surer for this was no longer unknown territory, and Wrynn helped to show them the way.

They sped along so that the walls were a blur and only the strange sinuous movements of the Thrall Maker's flesh kept them in touch with what transpired above.

'Left fork,' Wrynn said. He spoke quickly and with as much concentration as he could muster, given the distractions that troubled him. These others would come to experience it too, once the Radiant Iron had fully assimilated itself into their bodies: for there was only the one corpus of metal – all of the Radiant Iron that existed or ever would exist formed a single unified substance throughout time and space. And since it knew of itself, then all of those whose lives were touched by it would understand its intelligence too.

'Left fork again. Right fork – ah!'

The mage staggered back and his eyes glazed over for a moment. He righted himself, gesturing Kell away as the boy moved forward to help him.

'No matter . . . the dragon has been rent asunder . . . no matter. It will reconstitute itself again in time. Concentrate now – right fork. Right fork once more . . .'

Wrynn's commands were crisp and determined, but Sebalrai knew (as they all did deep inside themselves) that the enemy had gained the upper hand and were breaching Hugauga's defences. Soon the tunnels would be infested with hostile ships and what those ships contained – Slean, the armoured quasi-humans of the kind that had captured Shamra. Soldiers of the Sustren and the Goddess's unquestioning minions.

'But they can be killed,' he said softly, so that only Skjebne heard him and took some strength from the words.

Seconds later the travel orb swept into the great cavern of impossible stairways, and those aboard found it changed. Most of the dwelling-places were sealed over with slabs of the Radiant Iron; indeed the walls themselves were turning blue-grey as the metal rose up through the stone to form an impenetrable shield.

'My friends the villagers will hide themselves far within the secret galleries. The entire landscape would need to be ripped from the face of the planet to force them out now! And the fields of influence here will work to our favour. Keep the orb moving ahead as fast as you can Skjebne, and let the subtle fields carry us towards safety.'

Skjebne found this to be an act of great faith. His every instinct was to steer the orb both manually and mentally, since like the *Skymaster* itself, the smaller sphere responded to his thoughts. But Wrynn had asked him to trust, and so (with a rather nauseous grin) he lifted his hands away from the controls and allowed his mind to settle – only to jump with shock the next instant as the travel orb hurtled towards the cavern wall before swinging aside at the very last split-instant to vanish into a smaller side tunnel.

This headlong rush continued for several minutes, and the passengers almost grew used to the huge, gentle, powerful guidance of the fields that plummeted them down and along the narrowest of passageways, and then sent them swooping in great wide arcs through the other vast caverns they encountered.

In one such space they caught sight of several Slean craft at the opposite extreme, moving like bright shards of glass from a just-shattered window. Acting together, the ships changed course immediately without breaking formation and came on with dizzying speed, their guns loosing bolts of blue-white fire.

'Let me evade them!' Skjebne yelled, his confidence in the Thrall Maker having now reached its limit. But Wrynn's face was set and intent, and as the energy fields in the cavern took new hold of the orb and shot it into a tunnel, so it whirled and spiralled around the Slean ships and threw them apart like leaves on a turbulent sea.

'How long can we outrun them?' Kell wondered aloud. He had given up looking at the portal and the maps on the screen; both made him feel dizzy and sick. Just behind him Sebalrai was strapped securely into her seat, her defiance plain to see despite the paleness of her skin. Tsep had vanished into Kell's tunic pouch and was making not a murmur.

'Imagine a spider's web,' Wrynn told him by way of reply. 'Imagine a second tilted at right angles to it, the two interpenetrating. Imagine a thousand more all weaving together like an incredible sphere of strands. Now you begin to understand the complexity of Hugauga. Over millennia the Radiant Iron has spread outwards from its point of creation. The wrights who are descended from the Iron's originators predict that it will eventually grow throughout the whole planet – the consequences of this outcome being entirely unknown. But that is not even a problem for the sons of our sons! For now let us be content that we are alive and that the magical metal protects us.'

'Or hopefully protects us.' Skjebne was studying the luminous maps on the screen.

All around them attack ships were converging for the kill. They appeared as tiny many-pointed stars. Most of them were negotiating nearby tunnels, but a handful sped along the same passageway as the orb; three, four of them to the rear, and two approaching from up ahead.

'Why haven't the fields destroyed them?' Kell asked.

'Nothing is all-powerful,' the Thrall Maker said. 'Except perhaps for Wierd. And who knows but that it is Wierd's wish now that some of these Slean make it through.'

'But –'

'You might as well ask why the wind blows.' Wrynn smiled kindly on the boy, for he had asked these questions many times in his own youth; indeed he was still asking them, and still listening patiently for a reply.

'Let us seize the moment before our enemy can. Now Skjebne, if I read these luminescent charts aright, we will arrive at this juncture before any Slean ships catch actual sight of us.'

'That seems likely . . .'

'Then I suggest that we disembark there, and –'

'No, no.' Skjebne gave a small laugh half of annoyance and half at the absurdity of the plan. 'There is simply not time to slow down and lower the hatch before we are caught.'

'You mistake my intention. I am saying that we should keep the orb moving just as quickly as it moves now. The energies that guide it will take our momentum and carry us into the left-hand passage. The orb will continue on into the right, and there will meet its destruction at the hands of the Slean.'

It was a bold idea, and Wrynn reassured the others that the only danger in it lay in their own frightened minds.

Unexpectedly perhaps Sebalrai was the first to agree. She appreciated fully that they had but moments to act, and now positioned herself in front of the still-sealed hatchway ready to leap away.

Kell quickly joined her so as not to lose face in front of a girl. Skjebne favoured Wrynn with his wryest of glares, then took up his place behind Kell.

'We must all go together,' he told Wrynn. 'Stand close and I'll release the hatch locks.'

No sooner had his mind formed the thought than the hatch folded down in the face of a screaming blast of wind that almost plucked Sebalrai from the ship. Kell grabbed her tightly.

'Go! Go now!' the Thrall Maker yelled. And in an instant the younglings had vanished, followed by Skjebne and the mage.

None of them saw the orb swoop out of sight. The world was a howling storm of wind and noise and whirling grey rock streaked with colour . . . Then a darkness as they flew into the left-branching tunnel; a featureless blackness that made the sensation of speed all the more frightening and immediate.

Far away behind them they heard a strange whistling shriek as the Slean ships flashed past the tunnel entrance and a few heartbeats later felt a dull detonation deep in the earth as the orb was destroyed. Then, blessedly, their terrific velocity started to diminish; the maelstrom subsided and it was as though they were drifting along on the softest of cushions – but cushions woven from the thin air itself, for it was perfectly possible for any in the group to put out a hand and feel nothing beneath, or the brisk scrape of rough rock at their side.

'Remind me not to argue with you in future, Wrynn,' Skjebne said with a chuckle. His words might have sounded effusive, but Kell recognised they were spoken in relief. He was soaring along, as light as wisp, experiencing a wonderful buoyancy of spirit that came from truly giving himself up to fate, to the unfathomable workings of Wierd. For the first time in many seasons the future did not bear down upon him and force him to carry its burden on his shoulders. In this quietly gentle pocket of time, Kell was allowed simply *to be*; and the mystery of *Skymaster* and the horror of the Goddess and the Slean could wait awhile until later.

Their journey continued for a time they were unable to measure. And during that interval, a most remarkable thing happened. The Thrall Maker started to glow. It was so faint and so subtle at first that Wrynn's companions doubted their eyes. He was there, paler than a wraith, and not there; just an image lightly impressed on the mind. But gradually, and then more powerfully, the ghostly radiance emanated from him; from his robes, from his hands and his face. He was a spectral figure cast in moonlight, but with the absence of the moon.

'The Iron,' he said delightedly, turning without effort to look at his friends, 'lives up to its name.'

Before very long the walls too gave out a soft effulgence as though in response to Wrynn's state – and to her enormous joy Sebalrai began to master the art and caused her own hand to shine palely, as though held up into the beam of a distant ligetu lamp.

'As you come to know the metal and its properties within you – and as the Radiant Iron likewise learns – you will find it can serve you in many valuable ways. It has been the same with you since your discovery of the great Orbs, I suspect.'

'Just as you say,' Skjebne muttered rather absently, because a thought had occurred to him that sent a sharp pang of longing through his chest. For months now he had suffered weakness and pain in his leg, up close to the hip, where he had been stabbed during the madness in Perth. Could it be, could it possibly be, that the particles of Iron might undo that damage and give his bones full strength again . . . ?

Skjebne put the idea aside since he hated disappointment more than any other emotion, apart from regret. And shortly after he forgot it entirely, because the gentle grip of the fields changed around them. They came to a halt and experienced the illusion of the tunnel floor rising up slowly to receive them.

'I think we are safe for the present,' Wrynn said. 'The Iron inside me feels settled. But we must not become complacent. Although the Slean would find it nigh on impossible to destroy Hugauga and annihilate all its peoples, they could still do enormous damage and, if they found us, would wipe us out immediately.'

'So do we hide then?' Kell demanded to know with an edge of challenge in his voice. He was showing bravado on the surface because of his uncertainty inside. The thought that Hora and Fenrir had been slaughtered appalled him; he could not face it. And for the *Skymaster* to have been overcome so easily cast a bleak shadow on their aim to reunite with Feoh and Shamra. If the Goddess was so powerful, then they stood no chance at all.

Wrynn replied as though nothing was amiss. 'We will avoid the Slean until they tire of searching. Then we will make our way to Kairos. Unfortunately the fields do not extend beyond Hugauga. But there are outlying settlements where we can find transport – and a mwl's back is not so hard, once you have got used to it . . .'

Sebalrai saw the mischief in the mage's eyes and hid her smile. Certainly the situation was dangerous, but she knew that Wrynn was not about to lose his humour and sink into profitless worry. Besides, his lightness of soul gave her confidence, so that she realised that while dear Kell and Skjebne recognised Wierd, Wrynn had gone further and lived his whole life by its ways.

They walked on, although 'walked' did not truly describe the experience of taking easy steps that carried them for many spans at each stride. Upon reaching a spherical room in the rock, the group was met by a company of Hugaugans; small, pale, even-natured people who offered them refreshment and a choice of formidable-looking weapons which they gratefully, though nervously, accepted.

Then they moved on; randomly as far as the lack of landmarks was concerned, but obviously following the mage's clear sense of direction. Their path took them upwards, ever upwards; and even when the angle of the rock floor steepened to the point where they would ordinarily have needed to climb, they found the going easy and their footing firm and sure.

'Not far now,' Wrynn said presently. And in answer to the question they did not have time to speak, a cold fall of air began to spill past the travellers' faces bringing with it smell of the night. They must be close to the surface – And more! – And the mage must have known! Because as the Thrall Maker and then his companions stepped out into pale fitful moonlight, a burst of excited wulfenthoughts cascaded into Kell's mind.

Fenrir and his friends were alive.

The *Skymaster* had returned.

As quickly and as automatically as a reflex, the Thrall Maker's radiance faded and he became a shadow again. Sebalrai followed suit with swift common sense. Then the group crouched low to the ground.

'The great Orb must be somewhere quite near,' Kell whispered after explaining his realisation of its return. 'And Fenrir knows we are alive . . .' He chuckled at the wulf's cub-like joy in finding his friend again. 'But they don't know exactly where we are.'

'We must be careful,' Wrynn said, though the others needed no telling. A thin cold wind had risen as the temperature had dropped. Clouds were streaming fast across the sky, tumbling the darkness and light, while nearby the close-to-freezing air went hissing through the scrubthorn . . . No large noise of battle could be heard; the thunderous detonations from the dragon guardians had ceased now. But the air was filled with little sounds and disturbances – Yes, maybe the purposeless wind; but was that a clatter of stones to the right? And there, not far behind, was it someone treading softly crushing the ice-bleached grass?

They all felt the tension. Sebalrai snuggled closer to Kell and looked up at him and her eyes were lit by the sky's delicate iridescence.

'How do we tell Hora where we are?'

'I can keep my thoughts open to Fenrir. He'll pinpoint us in time.'

'For now,' advised Skjebne, 'we should seek more substantial shelter.'

'There are rocks not far away.' Wrynn's robes rustled as he stood. 'Follow me.'

They were pleased to do so: the wind was ruthless and already they felt their flesh numbed by its bite. They moved as quickly as they dared given the uncertain and ever-changing light and the pitfalls of the difficult ground. The scrubthorn lashed them as they passed by and up-thrust stones threatened to trip them almost at every stride.

But ahead, no further than a hundred paces, an outcrop of sandstone rose like a long-ruined temple. And close beside it stood a lower, more regular shape which might have been a great convex boulder deposited there in times long past by the receding glacial ice . . .

Might have been, but was not.

As the four travellers struggled towards it the pressure changed all around them: the shape seemed to activate and burgeon with life: it suddenly took on a dim and metallic lustre before erupting with light –

Kell cried out. Skjebne staggered backward and stumbled –

The Slean ship became instantly aware of the intruders. Its hull was suddenly astir with movement, as a score of insectile devices unfolded their spidery legs and began pattering quickly to the ground.

With a yell of warning Wrynn reached into his robes and swung up the weapon the Hugaugans had given him. He did not bother to take careful aim and a second later a great wash of strangely coloured flame surged across the black screens of scrub and swept them up into a barrier of fire.

Kell turned to run, thinking this was an opportunity for them all to take cover. But the mage's voice rang out again commandingly, accompanied by a lash of thought for him to stand firm for the moment.

Once Skjebne had steadied himself, he too hefted the fire-hurler and added to the Thrall Maker's diversion.

'They are simple creatures – atom-brained!' He laughed loudly and sprayed the air beyond the flame curtain with ever more liquid light. Even so three of the insects burst through the defences, two of them already burning. The third took several wavering steps and then stopped as though frozen. A harsh snapping sound crackled from inside its carapace. It jolted, twitched, and pitched forward on to the ground, its spindly limbs settling.

'The *hyrnetu* are often persistent but they have their

weaknesses . . .' Wrynn began walking backwards drenching the earth with flame. The other two slaves, ablaze like firebrands, came striding forward purposefully at first but then with swiftly decreasing co-ordination. Suddenly one fell like a toppled structure of sticks: its companion battled on for a moment or two until it succumbed to the heat and burst apart, its smoking components spinning and spattering all around in the underbrush.

Kell gave a whoop of triumph and excitement. Wrynn turned and stepped up to him and adjusted the settings on his weapon.

'Aim high,' he advised. 'Unlike men, these mechanisms learn from the death of their kind.'

The mage made similar alterations to his own fire-hurler. He pointed the barrel above the blazing wall and loosed a shining ball of flame as yet another hyrnetu sprang on high, clearing the danger.

Kell needed no second telling. His past practice with Skjebne had conferred a speed and elegance upon his muscles that hardly required his mind's direction. Acting on a sure reflex he tucked the stock of the hurler into his shoulder and fired off a stream of shining pellets as more of the insect slaves bounded the firewall and arced into view.

So their strategy settled briefly into a pattern as Skjebne and Sebalrai maintained the barricade of fire, while Kell and the mage picked off the hyrnetu that leaped out above it. Once and twice and three times a creature successfully landed within a few paces of the steadily retreating group: Wrynn broke off from his marksmanship and dispatched it instantly with another variation of the hurler's ability – a lance of light that he used to cut the slaves into so many smouldering pieces.

But their numbers were great and their determination was endless. A fourth hyrnetu bounded over the firewall and dropped to a crouch not five paces from its enemies. Kell loosed a round and smashed the slave back into the raging conflagration. A fifth landed, and Wrynn's firelance sundered its head from its body –

But then there were three more of the insects – six – ten – And beyond them a group of lumbering shadows that passed through the tapestries of flame as though they were no more than morning fogs: armoured Slean warriors moving in for the kill.

'Get back! Get back!' Wrynn yelled to the others. 'Run now – run for your lives!'

'Where's the orb? Kell, where is it!' Skjebne placed himself in front of Sebalrai and held his fire-hurler firm, though there was little point in using it now. The Slean seemed impervious to the heat; and while a few of the slave-insects collapsed on the fringes of the fires, more and more came to replace them, springing over the blaze or working a wide way around it.

A moment later Kell too desisted, and finally Wrynn let his weapon drop and laid it on the ground where it lay clicking as its metals cooled.

'Use your gift of vanishment.' Skjebne turned to the girl and saw the fear in her eyes and tried not to reflect it in his own. 'You can escape from them if you are lucky.' He noted that the cliff edge was near and stepped up to it carefully to assess her chances of survival. And he felt a great lifting of his heart at the sight of what was rising from the valley.

Kell . . .

Be still Skjebne. That was Fenrir's mindvoice, speaking

perhaps through the boy. *Do nothing but be patient for another few moments.*

It may have been that Wrynn too detected the change in his companions' demeanour. He glanced at them curiously before returning his attention to the Slean. Kell dashed his own fire-hurler almost contemptuously down, and Skjebne and Sebalrai followed suit, feigning surrender to buy a handful of time.

The armoured ones had walked clear of the burning ground and stood together gazing eyelessly at these fragile scraps of flesh that they were about to annihilate completely. One lifted its head at the flickerings among the clouds – the companion ships gathering above for what was intended to be a final assault upon Hugauga. Then its attention focused again on the cowering group of four and it considered the many ways that it possessed to destroy them . . .

Something huge rose up beyond the cliff edge, out of the valley and the night. At first it was no more than a darkness, a hull of shadow. But even as the Slean marauders tried to gather their simple wits to understand it, the sphere took on a faintly translucent glow and revealed a shimmering pattern of facets like a jewel cleverly worked.

One of the Slean raised its hand and released a pulse of force. Ordinarily it was enough to shatter rocks, but the vessel simply absorbed the blast and the assault came to nothing at all.

The other warriors stood indecisively. And the night turned into day, and for Kell and his friends it was as though the whole scene of the fire-lashed ground and the scurrying hyrnetu slaves, the ominous Slean and the danger they brought was swirled like paint in a whirlpool of water.

Their shapes and colours became meaningless and were spun around and sucked down into a fathomless hole, through which the whole universe followed.

6

The Time Of The Rad

'I did not know you were clever enough,' Skjebne said. It was intended to be another light-hearted snipe; but he was exhausted and shocked and in pain from the ordeal, and his voice came out weary and flat. He slumped down in a seat in the room of controls and half-closed his eyes.

'For once your faith in me is misplaced.' Hora smiled and rested his hand on Skjebne's thin shoulder. The man smelled of smoke and scorched ground. 'I stood here like a child at the heart of the miracle that was happening around me. I touched nothing.'

Fenrir moved up beside Kell and brushed his sleek flank against the boy's hip.

The Skymaster's *intelligence has reached a new level of activity. The – Slean – ships came at us like a fall of sky stones. We saw them also attacking Hugauga. The Wrym appeared –* And here the wulf's impressions grew darker and bloody and contained ideas that Kell did not understand nor would care to.

You must make brothers of your tolerance and wisdom, wulfensweor, Kell replied, *for the dragon-metal is within us.* He went on to recount their first meeting with Wrynn and his gift of the Radiant Iron, his thoughts skipping like a flat stone on water, touching the tale lightly in places.

The myth of the Draca is the marrow in our bones. Fenrir's gold eyes were wide and dark and intense. *But what does prophecy know? We are the lords of the moment!*

Nearby, Hora in his own way was trying to explain what had happened.

'The whole sky seemed to be shining. I was inside the crystal room and the walls were like weorthan gone insane! I saw the *Skymaster* from many views and angles. I saw you, my *geferan*, inside the travel orb – then outside tumbling away into the dark tunnel. There was a blinding light. The crystal room was awash with it!'

'*Sweorian*, Hora. Be calm. The *Skymaster* was looking with all its eyes at once. Its mind was working quickly to understand the situation – quicker than any of our minds, I'll wager.'

'But the shining sky, Skjebne!'

'Something happened which I can describe but don't understand. Right at the end, on the brink of the cliff when the Slean would have obliterated us by fire, we were snatched away by a hand both powerful and gentle; it was the hand of man but just as truly the hand of Wierd, something like the encompassing forces that cushion us in the crystal room and protected us along the rocky tunnels in Hugauga. An energy that is not bound as we are to what is here now . . .'

'The whole of Hugauga is protected by such subtle influences,' added Wrynn. 'The Draca uses them to move its many transforms through the tunnels and the sky.'

'Whatever it was, we were snatched out of space and held in an all-enfolding light. This light.'

Hora pointed to the viewscreens. They now showed a uniform brilliance that occasionally tantalised the watchers by revealing the intention of one shape or another, which invariably melted back into the featureless matrix: the wraiths of might-have-been.

'It is the light of the Rad.' The idea came into Kell's head like the morning, with effortless ease. 'That must be it. All of the great orbs surely have this capability . . . yes – yes – they can move from the sea to the mountains by crossing the distance. But there is another way – *by ignoring the distance . . .*'

'He's been smoking too much *wyrtegemang*!' Hora bellowed loudly, because the prospect frightened him so much. But Wrynn and Skjebne saw the sense of it.

'There is a great deal in what the boy says.' The mage again studied the light on the screens. 'I have heard other Thrall Brothers tell of a similar shine. It was common in the early days, in the times of glory, out of which came Hugauga's enshrouding fields and the Radiant Iron. Once I saw the Draca fly in a swarm across the night heavens and vanish in front of my eyes into a misty auroral glow. And occasionally during the ritual of Gebedraedan, especially when the festival is thronged, the atmosphere *hints* that such energies exist all around us.'

'Then that is the meaning of the Sigel Rad. Hora don't you see? The Rad is not the path the sun follows, but a reference to the very light that guides and nurtures. It is what links all of the filaments of life's weaving – it is Wierd's cloth, and we can go from any stitch to any other.'

'All very well,' the wyrda man blustered. His red hair and whiskers made his face look all the paler. 'But where are we now?'

And it was left to Kell to sum up what his mentors had reasoned and which opened the way to the future.

'Wherever we want to be, Hora. Wherever is our true heart's desire.'

In the far mountains, in Uthgaroar, in the chamber of the eolders, on the other side of the shadow, Thorbyorg and the rest of the council watched the Universal Wheel spin with a terrifying speed. It moved soundlessly in a blur of dark metals lit by occasional sparks. No part of it held still long enough to be defined by any eye, and yet the whole formed a picture, an abstract, of such beauty and truth that the eoldermen gathered there never once feared for their safety or the souls of their children and wives.

Inside the Room of Decisions, the road to the future was clear.

Leofsonu the cynic weighed up the extent to which his life was freighted with sin, and came to the conclusion that this mattered less than the dust.

'I can feel the spinning inside me,' he whispered, welcoming the Wierd. Another of the *ealdbeorn* said, 'This is the light of the Rad,' in hushed and reverent tones. The revelation was unfolding in the minds of many men –

At which point the wheel stopped utterly but for the minute shiftings of one or two interior rings.

There was a gasp from the council. A few looked to Thorbyorg for guidance.

Garulf, the First Eolder's assistant, came bustling in.

'Lord! Lord! The *Skymaster* has returned. But it came in a blaze like . . . like . . .'

'Like the sun, *genera*. We know. Put your fear aside now Garulf. Go and rouse all the families in the settlement, and tell the men of the Wyrda Craeftum to be ready to travel with them, or to say their goodbyes. I shall select from the ranks very shortly.'

Thorbyorg turned back to his councillors and noted that their faces – aye, bearded scarlet and grey and lined with age and the lash of many storms – seemed as open and innocent as children's now, at the prospect of stepping off the brink of what had always been comfortable and safe . . .

'From what our good friends Kell and Skjebne have said, any one of the Great Orbs can carry Uthgaroar's entire population. But my thinking is that the people should be divided and borne along in two of them, leaving *Skymaster* and one other for the battle that is surely just below the horizon. Three of you will travel in each of the departing orbs and be the wisdom and the comfort of the people . . .' Thorbyorg could not help but chuckle at the consternation his comment caused. 'Pretend you can do it.' He added with a gleam, 'and your hearts will take strength and follow.'

'But where are we going?' Leofsonu wanted to know. 'And what will we do when we get there?'

'I cannot tell you who will stand on the farther shore to greet you and help you unload your boat. Nor, indeed, do I know what place marks the end of the Rad. But you know as I do that our distant fathers and mothers journeyed out and that our fondest heart's wish has been to follow them. That opportunity has now been given to us and we must embrace it fully. Go there in peace in the name of all our kind, and tell them of the brave ones who will not be coming home.

'Now, *eolderman*, go about your business. Garulf – fetch Zaurag and instruct him to bring the Wheel. I must meet Kell and his friends at the threshold.'

★

The wind had risen with the night and came whistling up from the deep valleys and away over the tops. Hearth fire smoke whipped about the roofs and turned to nothing as soon as the eye could catch sight of it. Thorbyorg pushed open the sturdy oaken door and grunted at the chill blast that ambushed him around the corner of the hearth hall, and shrugged his furs more closely around himself.

The stars were spilled dusts across the cold crystal dark. Normally the First Eolder would have taken time to appreciate them. But the moment was filled with urgency; and besides something more astonishing had caught his attention.

The previously inert hulls of the triune orbs, *Windhover*, *Cloudfarer*, *Heavenwalker*, had come alive with a gentle glow; a soft radiance of blue and green and subtle silver that played about the metal. Higher up, closer to, *Skymaster* burned with a bolder light of yellow and gold and sporadic streaks of red. And as though the watching eyes of its passengers had noticed Thorbyorg upon the instant of his appearance, the orb swiftly descended and the air hummed with life and the ground was filled with profound energies.

The First Eolder stood firm because he knew that many of his people would be watching. He was the symbol of their purpose, a man unflinching as the heavens came down to meet him. And not just human eyes looked on. Magula and the other wulfen of Fenrir's pack peeped out from their clefts in the rocks and drew wonder from the fact that one of their own rode the sun.

Skymaster swooped close and stopped on the instant,

with the same suddenness as the Wheel. The hatchway gestured down and the travellers emerged – Fenrir leaping away to greet his kind; then Hora who bowed to his *eolderman* and grinned with boyish pride in his achievement. Kell and Sebalrai came next, and it was then that Thorbyorg noticed the rare pallor of their skin: this had touched Hora too, though his scarlet hair and beard had hidden its effect. Skjebne was also tainted (though he walked with unexpected energy and a confident tread), and behind him stood a tall and exotic stranger, surely Wrynn the mage, of whom Kell had spoken – and just as surely the cause of the others' transformation.

Skjebne stepped lightly down from the orb and made his introductions. Thorbyorg pulled his broad hand free from its moxenfur mitten and had the wisdom not to draw it back as Wrynn's pale fingers, grey as lead, touched his own and clenched them in a strong and confident grip.

'If I had as much time as curiosity, *frio*, I would remember my manners and offer you hospitality; and forget them again as I questioned the tincture of your skin.' Thorbyorg glanced again at the sky. 'But I think that both doom and salvation are upon us, like the bright and shadowed faces of the moon.'

'Your wisdom is well rooted, First Eolder,' Wrynn said and the compliment came with a diplomat's ease. 'My imagination made a picture of complacency and sloth, but I see that you have anticipated the arrival of the Slean and are already making preparations to escape them.'

'That is the sum of it, aye.' Thorbyorg beamed with pleasure, but there was a nervous little creasing of his brows because neither Kell nor Skjebne nor anyone else had told

97

him much of these marauders or the exact threat they posed. 'Needless to say I have mobilised my people who will soon be ready to leave.'

'This is the time then?' Hora looked humbled. 'The time of the Rad?'

'For many of the clan, yes indeed. But the Wyrda's strength is still needed here, for while the Goddess exists she might follow us.'

Briefly Thorbyorg explained his plan while the new-comers walked with him to his rooms where he donned his war gear. This included embossed metal plate to armour the back and the chest, and hardened leather arm and leg shields decorated with the runes and sigils of the Wyrda Craeftum. Then from a secret niche covered over with a cloth, Thorbyorg withdrew a magnificent helmet that looked to be made of the same dark metal as the orbs; crude grey iron at one moment, but then with a shift of perception or the merest tilt of the light it seemed to gleam like a skim of oil upon water, and all the rainbow's colours and some more besides could be seen there.

'It is the Guardian Helmet,' announced Thorbyorg loftily. 'Symbol of the Wyrda Craeftum, defenders of the Rad.'

'And is it nought but a helmet?' Skjebne wanted to know, having noticed the peculiar play of the firelight over its surface.

The First Eolder paused in putting it on, and there was a certain wryness and regret in his reply. 'If it is more, then I have never possessed the wit to discern it. Like the Wheel itself it has always been regarded as a sacred thing; and deep mysteries have been suspected in its crafting . . . But if it keeps my head warm and deflects a blow or two from a

Slean axe, it will have served its purpose as far as I am concerned!'

'Well, I think the invaders will bring worse weaponry than that.' Wrynn kept his misgivings to himself – and his anger. He had heard of the Wyrda Craeftum and admired the nobility of their purpose. But here on this mountain he found only a settlement of ignorant *ceorls* clinging to the decayed remains of an all-but-forgotten tradition. Luckily it seemed that the Orbs were more advanced than the Slean ships, which must cross half a continent to reach their destination. It might be some little time before they arrived, and perhaps that would be long enough to see these people away safe.

Garulf was on hand to strap Thorbyorg securely into his armour, and shortly afterwards Zauraq appeared bearing the Wheel, with Verres standing solidly at his side. The huge boar snuffled around Wrynn's legs and opened its mouth to show the stranger its fearsome fighting teeth. It had detected the tension and the uncertainty in its master, and its own heart had felt the unique touch of fear; and so the boar's anger was close to the surface to mask the fear, as a defence against that which could not be fought.

'Let Zauraq take the Wheel into the Orb, Eolder,' Skjebne advised. 'You will need it for your journey more than we will require its guidance here.'

Thorbyorg weighed his options. 'I agree with you, friend. You will continue to be the keeper of the Wheel, Zauraq. Go aboard *Heavenwalker* now and let stout Verres remain at your heel . . . Garulf, I want you too to enter the sanctuary of the Orb.' The boy hesitated: he had been raised from an infant to serve the First Eolder even to the point of offering his life before he would see Thorbyorg come to any harm. And now to be ordered away like this, cursorily dismissed without explanation.

'*Eodor*, I would prefer it if –'

'Go now! That is my final instruction to you!'

And Thorbyorg stood firm and proud and unmoving as the face of his lifelong genera crumpled like a child's, and Garulf bowed, his eyes filled and shining, and a moment later turned his back on his lord and ran from the room.

'Now I will inspect my men! And we will drive these putrid Slean from the skies!'

Thorbyorg's voice was too loud, too strident. Skjebne caught Kell's attention with his gaze and then Wrynn's, and the men withdrew. Sebalrai came over to where the First Eolder was standing. She touched his wrist and her hand looked tiny against his.

'There is often pain in compassion. Garulf will come to see that one day.'

'Go along with the others, *bearn*,' Thorbyorg answered very quietly. 'I want my leavetaking to be a private thing.'

Sebalrai did as she was bidden and walked out into the night.

Within the past few minutes the two orbs, *Heavenwalker* and *Cloudfarer*, had drifted close to the ground. From each great ship a number of ramps had descended and wyrda warriors were ushering the citizens of Uthgaroar aboard; the fathers of the fathers, the women and children and even the animals that provided milk and meat. Then they would gather inside the crystal rooms for the *eoldermen* to explain this most extraordinary of nights. And even as that explanation was given, the light of the Rad would wash them away to the distant shores of this incomparable sea.

Midway between the streams of people Zauraq stood

holding the Universal Wheel aloft. The light spilling out of the orbs showed the spinning of its rings, an indication that the ways of Wierd were much more complex than men could easily follow.

As the crowds diminished and the thoroughfare grew quiet, the wulfen crept out from their places in the rocks. *Heavenwalker* and *Cloudfarer* withdrew with less sound than a sigh, and *Windhover* approached, its spherical hull defined by a gentle shimmering of light.

The thought was yours, Fenrir, that you could use the orb to find other forests. Your pack has nurtured me and taught me much; and you and Magula have been among my finest friends. Kell knelt down so that the young princeling wulf could be level with him eye to eye. *I offer you that chance now, as a gift in return. Soon the Slean will arrive and devastate this place. But we can all be gone from here by then. The other slow-eyes and I will travel to Kairos and then on to Arcanum for our confrontation with the All Mother. You wulfensweor and the others of the pack can find the green refuge you dream of and be safe there and happy for all the rest of your seasons.*

Fenrir looked upon the boy and noted the growth of man-hair on his chin and the greater confidence of his mind, and the adult complexity and depth of his intentions. Somewhere below the surface of Kell's thoughts lay some of the treasures of the wulfenhoard. Hidden among them the apocalyptic vision of the Fenrir wulf driving the humankind out of the world through a torn and bloody sky. No one, not even perhaps the soul of Wierd, fully understood the symbolism of that scene, nor when it would be enacted. Kell's offer now was possibly a way of putting off that fateful time when wulfen jaws were clamped around a mortal throat. Or maybe the boy simply did not wish to see his friends' bodies cleaved open by Slean blades. Maybe Kell was as innocent as he seemed.

Fenrir kept all of these wonderings to himself, hiding them cleverly away. He felt glad that Kell's concentration was elsewhere, fixed on Sebalrai and the bustle of the leavetaking.

We are of one mind. All of the male wulfen, and those bitch wulves who are young enough yet without cubs, will fight by your side. You have brought us far in our understanding of the slow-eyes, Kell. That may be a blessing or a bane for you or for me or for both of us . . . Also, we will never forget the risk you took in finding us shelter in Edgetown among Alderamin's kin. And, most significantly for me, you stayed your hand in Thule when your instincts told you to drive the knife through my heart. All of these things prompt us to stay with you now. We will come with you to Arcanum and face the Goddess together.

This entire exchange had occurred in a flicker of time; so that it seemed the boy had barely knelt to stroke the wulf's pelt when he stood again and nodded to his friends and announced that the pack would fight beside them.

And now the radiance of the further orbs was increasing as *Heavenwalker* and *Cloudfarer* drifted higher in the sky. A haze of mist was forming around them fading out the stars.

'The orbs themselves have judged the time,' Skjebne said. 'Maybe all of this was laid down in the Wheel's configurations . . .' Maybe we are like puppets dancing to another's tune, he thought, a rebel echo in his head. And the pride we take in our free will is only a weorthan dream . . .

The orbs' light increased to an unbearable brilliance before fading back to a ghostly glow. Their appearance now was uncertain, as though some part of the mind believed they were there, while another part knew without doubt they had gone. Around them the pinpoint light of the stars as smeared out into delicate streaks and swirls. Thin cloud was being whisked away into nothingness. Dust and even small stones stirred on the ground about the onlookers' feet and went scurrying this way and that all in unison like particles trapped in a magnetic tide.

Then something changed and *Cloudfarer* was no longer hanging in front of their eyes. There was no glorious departure. The orb had simply ceased to be. *Heavenwalker* followed seconds later, giving Kell time to anticipate its vanishing. And he came to wonder at the pattern of his thoughts that divided here from there and then from this instant. Because suddenly it seemed to him as though the whole work of Wierd had started from now and left traces behind . . . Like Alderamin might once have scratched marks on his story stones, that written record, that seeming past, is still and only now.

These ideas were too huge or too elusive for Kell to hold in his head. Sebalrai gasped at the sight of the orbs' disappearance, and his concentration wavered and then he had forgotten what he'd thought, and was left only with the sense of its significance.

Windhover swung in low for Fenrir and the wulfen to enter.

'Let us be quickly away from here,' said Thorbyorg, for the houses and the heights felt very lonely to him now.

A thin and terrible shrieking came from somewhere far above. Fenrir's superior sight first spotted the molecule sailing fast among the stars. The sound of it, the awful screeching, was like claws being scraped along glass.

'Hurry – hurry!' urged Skjebne. A ramp folded down from the orb and Magula's powerful mindvoice encouraged his pack aboard.

Will you travel in Skymaster? Fenrir wanted to know.

Yes, we'll divide for safety. Are you coming with us, or –

Then there was no more communication between them. Something much closer than the trailing star had lofted the tops and was bearing down on them from behind. There came an angry crackling and a mighty roar and a clutch of houses and the settlement's hearth hall vanished in a flash as the ground beneath was ploughed up by a huge gout of fire.

The heat and wave of the blast caught them a second later. Kell was swept off his feet and saw his friends tumbling also. The Slean ship hissed by and dropped below their line of sight into the valley.

'Get up! Get aboard!' That was Skjebne's voice. He was unharmed. Kell heard men running and as he scrambled up saw wyrda fighters coming into view. He stood and cast round for Sebalrai, and there she was in Wrynn's care.

'Quickly now take her into the orb – and here.' He delved into his tunic and brought out the pouch within which Tsep lay hidden. The poor thing must be missing its quiet life in the Hreaomus caves! Kell thrust the pouch into the mage's hand and watched him ushering Sebalrai aboard *Windhover*. Then he looked for Fenrir and found him safe though dazed nearby.

These Slean have an animal's cunning. The wulf's lips were drawn back from the shock of the attack, although to Kell's human eye it looked as though he were grinning. *That ship will return very soon to complete its assault . . .*

But is its mission to destroy us completely, Kell

wondered, or does the All Mother know of our links with Uthgaroar – and does she wish to capture us alive?

Skjebne meanwhile was not troubling to reflect on the matter. Wrynn and Sebalrai had vanished into the body of the orb: the last wulfen likewise had entered, with the exception of Fenrir. The first of the wyrda rearguard were arriving at the ramp and Skjebne was encouraging them on.

'Come quickly inside. Be not afraid for this is wyrda ground. You will be safe in here . . .'

Thorbyorg was using a different tactic, bellowing commands as his warriors went by, spurring them forward with the whiplash of his voice.

We should follow the eolder's own good counsel. Fenrir directed Kell's attention with a shift of his mind. And almost immediately Kell spotted the Slean ship swooping back up out of the gorge, its hull reflecting faint gleams from the light of the orbs and the fires of its own creation.

It loosed a pulse of force – something hardly visible, as though its radiance existed beyond the limits of what the eye could see – and immediately another cluster of dwellings erupted into flame, and burning fragments of wood spiralled into the sky and fell all around in a blazing shower.

Fenrir yelped and Kell cut through the wulf's raw fear and urged him towards the threshold. The last wyrda soldier had already gone inside, though Thorbyorg himself stood back simply gazing at the ruin of his domain.

Kell ran across to the First Eolder and felt his pain, remembering Alderamin's agony when the drengs of the Tarazad had laid Edgetown to waste.

'Come with me now Thorbyorg. There is nothing for us here any more.'

'I will have my vengeance for this atrocity.' The

warrior's hand went to the axe at his hip but the boy forestalled him.

'Save your rage for the Goddess. These Slean are like insects obeying on blind impulse. They do not reason. They take no pleasure from this. Instead be glad that your people still live.'

The man's hard fist unclenched and slowly he nodded his head, the strange burnish of the Guardian Helmet catching the lick of the flames.

'Your cool reason is what I need most at this moment, Kell. Otherwise no doubt I would end up in cinders like Uthgaroar itself.'

He followed the boy into the orb – but at his own pace, refusing to hurry away.

And no sooner had the hatchway closed than *Windhover* soared in a heartbeat to a height that equalled the span between the river and the tallest mountain peaks.

Skjebne had gone at once to the crystal room, leaving the mind of the orb to know what to do for the best. From there he saw the landscape fall away and a small cluster of Slean craft swarm about in confusion above the burning wreckage of the town. It seemed no more than a tiny blaze kindled in a cup among the rocks; nothing at all within the wider world, but heart-home throughout history to the men of the Wyrda Craeftum.

But it seemed now that there were fewer craft than they had seen above Hugauga. And Skjebne took pleasure in knowing that the Draca had mustered an effective retaliation.

Standing beside him, but looking elsewhere, Sebalrai watched aghast as *Skymaster* began its transformation. Already the power had risen to its surface and swept through its fabric. The air and the starlight all around began to distort.

A Slean craft sped upwards and fired repeatedly; bolts of dark energy so blue-violet they were almost completely invisible. They appeared to have no effect whatsoever. And as the attack ship drew closer, *Skymaster* replied with a tendril of light that wove back down the sky and reached its target with an almost tentative touch –

The vessel and its every particle blazed up so brightly that the whole mountain range stood out starkly in the flash, and upon fading left its green ghost to haunt the eyes.

Sebalrai squealed and in her fright turned towards Skjebne. But she turned and turned and never found him, for existence was folding in upon itself like a crumpling cloth on which was drawn the entire landscape of her life.

The only time and the only place was that which the company could imagine for itself. The crystal room was too small to accommodate the occupants of the orb: Kell, Skjebne, Hora and Sebalrai patiently settled the new travellers into their chambers, and then returned with Thorbyorg, Wrynn and the wulfen elders to the crystal room to discuss their plans.

Outside the walls the true light of Wierd lapped like a featureless sea. Out of it had come the world and its one history, although every past and an infinity of futures existed there in potential. For a short while the group teased their own minds, imagining a variety of wonders looming out of the vast incandescence like shapes that begin to form themselves in clouds, only to change or come to nothing soon after. But presently, just as children grow bored with the mysterious commerce of adults, so the company turned in upon itself to deal with their own affairs.

'There is, of course, the one immediate goal of finding Feoh.' Wrynn cast a falcon's glare at Kell and Skjebne. Hugauga had been threatened and Uthgaroar devastated already since their meeting with the mage. Wrynn could not help but wonder if these people were more of a liability than an asset.

'I believe that is already decided,' Skjebne answered with equal formality. 'We are going to Kairos, and my hope is that we can bring Feoh within the sanctuary of the orb. Here we are out of the swing of the sea. I doubt that the All Mother can send her Slean to locate us –'

'But time moves on in the mortal world,' Thorbyorg reminded them, removing his helmet to speak his thoughts more clearly. 'Feoh is in danger now, and will be tomorrow, if we do not move to recover her. And then, Kell, there is your friend Shamra and the threat of the Goddess herself. That grows no less as we procrastinate.'

'True enough, true enough.' Skjebne leaned forward into the debate. 'But we cannot afford to rush headlong. See how we constantly learn more of the Orbs' marvellous powers. Despite the strength of your wyrda fighters Thorbyorg, we are a meagre force when set against the power of the Goddess. For all we know she broods over a hundred enclaves, or thousands, and upon her whim can hatch them out and send her armies against us!'

'Then let us strike before she does so,' Hora insisted.

Beside Kell Fenrir grunted. *They are like a gang of toothless, loose-dugged ealdmodoren*, he sneered.

Kell smiled at the idea and glanced at the wulf, and then across the way towards Sebalrai as she idly lifted up the

Guardian Helmet. Perhaps she was tired of the talk, or maybe mention of Shamra had touched a raw nerve; but almost playfully she tilted the helmet this way and that, beguiled by its light, and then slipped it over her head.

And started to scream.

7

A City Out Of Time

She knew that the strangers were coming.

Once – even so brief a time as a season ago – they would have approached her door unexpectedly. Now she sensed them afar in many ways. She could smell the man's disease; she could feel the girl's fear of contagion crawling in her own flesh; and with a deep yet factless knowledge she gathered up some scraps of information about the family's circumstances . . . He was a jeweller of some repute, but not highly regarded enough for patrons to bring him their most valuable metals and stones. She, his most precious treasure, was involved with a young man of dubious reputation and motives. Her mother, the dying man's wife, remained a shadowy figure shackled by the covenants of companionship, and almost glad that her life's pain would end with his passing . . .

Except that he could be saved. Feoh might have idled her time away collecting snippets like these until the patient arrived on her doorstep. Instead, with a gentle self-chiding, she busied herself about the room which was one half of her modest abode; setting the examination table with clean linens; arranging the ligetu lamps to cast a pool of bright light while draping the rest of the chamber in the privacy of shadows, making ready what few instruments she might need – an ocular glass, a fleen to draw blood (the locals occasionally insisted on this), and some coloured liquids and powders that served only the purpose of impressive effect.

She was ready and waiting as Wraecca and Anak turned the corner of that quiet street in Kairos to consult with Feoh the thaumaturge, whose miracles of healing were becoming well known throughout the under-culture of the city.

She opened the door as they knocked (Anak's knock, nervous and respectful) and beckoned them in with sweep of her hand and the merest of smiles. She noted that Wraecca was dressed in his best tunic of gat skin, formally buttoned to his neck. Anak wore a looser white silken shirt belted at the waist and bordered with bright embroideries.

Outside the sky's milky light was unchanging; it might have been day or night but Kairos existed in its own timeless fashion. Feoh smelt a brief whiff to the *wringe* press across the way, and in the next street someone was roasting ouzel meat on sticks as part of a birth celebration. She heard the more distant calling of a trinket seller announcing his wares to the rattle of a tambour: and the whisperings of all the millions of minds that seethed across the feldlands frightened her briefly until she turned her back on them and gave her visitors her full attention.

'Welcome to my house. How can I help you?'

The terror of agony and dying flashed through Wraecca's heart. But to Anak the woman seemed mysterious and powerful – capable in her ways. Surely she already knew what aid was required. Nevertheless the girl answered, 'My father has dreadful cramps in his stomach and is in constant pain. He coughs blood and cannot eat. The sickness is drawing the life out of him. We know of your abilities – you are called the Healer. Please, do what you can to save him now, Feoh.'

The older woman realised that her initial opinion of Anak had been wrong. She was not a pale ghost like her mother, but a brave and wilful girl who thought she knew her own path clearly and followed it with great determination. A name is a personal thing and manners require that it is offered: Anak had swept etiquette aside and used Feoh's name without permission, yet not without respect. She was a resourceful child to be sure.

To the father Feoh said, 'Lie down on the table and let me examine you.' Wraecca did so, lowering himself carefully so as not to outrage his pain. The skin of his face was grey-white and the bags beneath the eyes were as blue as a bruise. Feoh told Wraecca to open his tunic, then she felt his belly with a cool and gentle hand.

'There is something growing there, I know it. I can feel it,' he groaned. 'Will you need to bleed me?'

'Well, that might make a mess of your fine tunic, sir. Would you mind that?'

Wraecca hesitated, looking puzzled.

'Then tell me instead,' Feoh went on, 'Would you let your wife ignore your needs for a moonth or two?'

'What do you mean?'

'Can she now let the hearth fire go out and allow you to sleep in an unmade bed? Oh, Anak, I wonder if you would lend your mother your other best shirt – I know you have two. And Wraecca, something tells me you are working on a particularly fine jewelled brooch right now. I suggest that you substitute garnets for jade. Your wife, Etreo, prefers them. Give her the brooch with your love as a gift. Also, give her a generous bag of coin and let Anak take her about the city. Insist that they return with whatever they please, but with no money left at all, not a single *sceatt* . . .'

'This is outrageous!' Wraecca started to struggle up from the table. Feoh pushed him down with a firm palm and pressed his tight and swollen stomach until the man howled.

'This tumour is a strong and vigorous son to you, jeweller. But you have a daughter, a fine intelligent child who loves you. Be glad of that and be glad of your trade. Forgive Wraecca the offence of self-judgement and let Etreo enjoy herself in Anak's image before she considers herself too old and respectable to laugh or get drunk in a loud *winsael*.'

Again Wraecca complained and tried to rise. Feoh loomed down and brought her face close to his so that she could sniff the rancidness of his breath.

'Listen to me. If you do nothing you will be dead in a moonth. Nothing will have been achieved. Or you can pay me the ridiculous sum I will ask of you and I can take the cancer away. But it will return, Wraecca, to haunt you. Can't you hear it moaning already? It is the sound of rage and regret.'

Wraecca lay still like a trapped bird. He looked terrified. Feoh hauled him up.

'Look over there. That door leads to your future or the grave. Walk to it yourself. Do it now! Anak – stay here, for I would speak with you further.'

Almost weeping Wraecca hobbled and dragged himself across the room, turning as he reached the threshold.

'You have not heard the last of this!'

'Indeed I have, unless you change your mind.'

After Wraecca had gone, Feoh readjusted the lamps. Anak gave a little gasp that she tried to withhold, but too late.

'I'm sorry – I thought shadows . . .'

Feoh touched the cold ceramic that masked half of her face. She smiled wistfully.

'I am much better than I was. The damage does not go so deep now, but there are things to be done before the healing is complete . . . However we aren't here to discuss my destiny. Do you think your father will follow my counsel?'

The girl shrugged and smiled but looked uncertain. 'I'll do what I can to make sure he does.'

'Very good. And how much will you do for his sake?'

'Well –'

'Now, do not think of your boyfriend's name – ah, it is Thursta. What is your view of him?'

'I love him.'

'No you don't. You think he is shiftless and deceitful. But outwardly he appears bright and popular and he breathes through your life like a freshening breeze. But to him you are a jewel, an ornament he wears until a prettier one comes along – No, I won't stop it.' Feoh noticed the spark in Anak's eyes and knew it would be her salvation.

'You will not become the echo of your mother. You are stronger than that. But don't betray yourself by thinking that people like Thursta are your friends. Enjoy his company until he hurts you the first time, then walk away from him. Your choice too, the future or the grave.'

Now tears came into Anak's eyes, but she did not rant as Wraecca had done. Instead she nodded and reached into a pocket and gave Feoh the *sahfire* ring that Wraecca had judged as her fee.

'They say you are Sustren,' Anak said, almost shyly. 'Do you suppose my future lies in that direction?'

'I say you are a woman who loves the life of things. I think you will in time meet a man you love through and through, and your children will be handsome and will prosper. What can the Sustren give you better than that?'

Feoh opened the door for her guest and let the light spill inside.

'Be self-guided along the way.' She reached out and touched Anak's fair hair. 'I see that your first born will be a son, and he will be blonde. And you will pay for his birth celebration with a fine garnet brooch. Now go, for your father is waiting.'

Feoh watched Anak walk away until the girl reached the corner and did not look back. With a little effort, with some *prying* that she did so well these days, Feoh knew that she could discover the end of the tale that she and Anak and Wraecca had started today. But there were other stories waiting to be told, so most likely she would leave things be, taking comfort in the fact that she had shown both father and daughter how to author their fate, and through her skill may have saved at least one of them.

Now in timeless Kairos, Feoh felt a sudden urgency. It was a soft but insistent sensation that came to her first as a quickening of her heart for no reason that she could quite understand. The temptation to look around herself for clues was strong, but then she smiled as she recalled her own learning. This puzzle would solve itself by the time she had made herself ready.

Withdrawing into her apartment, she washed and combed out her hair and braided it with beaded cord.

Then she opened an ebony powder box, sprinkled some of the blue dust on to a soft pad infused with perfumed oil and carefully applied the cosmetic to her face, all the while ignoring the stark black gloss of the mask that through its addition took so much from her and saddened her heart.

Finally Feoh placed a jewel on her forehead which she adhered to her skin with a dab of resinous mix. It was a moonstone, tinted blue to complement her makeup but also to signify that although she was a single woman, her love was pledged. And then she understood the impulse that was directing her. More purposefully now she strapped a leather scabbard to her leg and sheathed the stabbing knife which was her everyday weapon of choice: she was Sustren and her art was respected, and Kairos was largely benign. But experience had taught her that the world was full of danger, and there were some in the city for whom their hatred of the Sisterhood far outweighed their fear.

Before leaving, Feoh went to a hidden niche in the wall and retrieved a small pouch. She upended it and a large blue gemstone tumbled out into her hand. Its colour was exquisite, far superior to Wraecca's sahfire ring. It was the *cristilla* that Alderamin had once presented to her, long ago, far away – a weapon of frightening potency which also contained a knowledge of its own destiny . . . was it the crystal, or was it Feoh's own racing imagination, that filled her with a sense of *imminence* just now? She smiled at the games that she played with herself, returned the gem to its bag and hung it from her neck by a thong.

Feoh wrapped a dark blue *hacele* around her and drew its caul over her head before stepping out into the street. Her home was one small ordinary house in a long row of the same; a modest box with boxes on the top in which the slightly wealthier people lived. They commanded a view of the much more imposing dwellings built at the foot of the hills to the west, and of the extensive palatial retreats where the Thrall Makers went about their work. She had been there a number of times, initially because of her healing abilities and then at Wrynn's invitation. She had seen something of the *drycraeft* being practised and it amazed her and frightened her equally. The most powerful enchanters, the *lyblaeca*, laid their hands on the body of Wierd as Feoh did on her sufferers. If the legends and the evidence of her own eyes were true, then they could feel the pulse of existence and direct the energy of life according to their will. The oldest and yet most excessive of the tales suggested that the Thrall Makers of ancient times had crafted the Seetus itself and planted the living seed of wisdom deep within its brain. Similarly they forged the wulfen and lodged within them the gift of synerthy to help them survive on the Ice. And the wulfen, it seemed, was but one product of the mages' esoteric art.

Feoh's scepticism squatted like a devil on her shoulder as Wrynn had recounted these fables. And yet she had seen some intriguing sights . . . Also was it not the case that the city had never existed under the ground? It had always stood proudly on the plains, surrounded and protected by its mists that made the city impervious to storms. And it was indeed undeniable that once under the influence of Kairos, beguiled by its *onweardnes*, time was not a drawn line but more like spilled water spreading on parchment; and the possibility that all things *could be so* unfolded strongly in the heart.

Feoh reviewed her impressions now and decided that Wrynn was most probably right. Through the Sustren the Goddess was a pervasive presence here – why else should it be except that the *lyblaeca* possessed the power over life and the flesh that she sought? Little Sister trapped in her cold lonely prison of glass longed to live again in the world. Perhaps only the makers of the Seetus and the wulfenkin's creators could achieve that aim.

Feoh's way took her through the busy trading quarter which reminded her so poignantly of Perth. Here too the merchants sold a huge profusion of items. Some of the sellers advertised their wares in clear strident tones, while others sat silent and absorbed in their craft of needlework or carving, fortune telling or· bead making or one of a thousand others. Most of the traders and passers-by ignored her or cast only a passing incurious glance. A few, more innocent or less mannered, stared openly at her facial mask with expressions of curiosity or revulsion in varying degrees. Once or twice people who were either gifted intuitives or simply suspicious gazed upon her darkly, cursing that she was Sustren; although the common feeling remained that the Sisters were not a bane in Kairos. They had brought much that was of value to the *straetfolc*, the common people. Mainly it was the Thrall Makers that disapproved, and then only those enchanters who had not yet fallen under the women's glamour.

For a time Feoh concentrated on these ideas, working them as she might chew a twist of tough meat. But the day was peaceful and pleasantly warm and the *gaest* of the streets was benign, and soon enough she let the conundrums go until they faded from her mind. Besides, the state of quiet awareness was the most useful in allowing her to know which way to walk – beyond the sprawling markets and on towards the hills, but tending away from the Thrall Makers' domain.

High on the uplands many winding paths led through featherbracken to viewpoints overlooking Kairos and the plains; or to clumps of chalky outcrop rock where light warm winds blew random tunes through the pipegrass, and where agate-bees sang. Here and there stood ancient ruins carved with fathomless glyphs. Feoh paused beside one such tilted slab of honeystone and let her mind relax, endeavouring to draw meaning from the runes. Nothing came, except an inkling that time was not a useful concept to apply to these stones. Perhaps some mischievous spirit had placed them here this morning, or maybe they predated the Ice and Kairos itself. It hardly mattered in the greater scheme of things. They were Wierd's whim, meaning nothing beyond themselves.

Now Feoh needed to shake off her mood of lethargy to continue. She felt tantalised by the nearness of understanding that seemed always one step ahead of her. It was like trying to realise the rain by taking hold of it, and she didn't know whether to feel amused or annoyed. Instead, she put both behind her and walked on, throwing back her caul and opening the hacele because there was no one else around and the air was fresh and sweet.

At last she came to a small dell where spires of rock stood at one end. A faint vapour like dawn mist poured between these columns, and by letting the eye linger there long enough it seemed that the haze was self-luminous and charged with potential.

Feoh had never been here before, but knew she had reached her destination. She had brought no food, though an apple tree grew nearby and its fruit looked nourishing and ripe. She plucked one and settled against the trunk with her cloak folded up to cushion the wood. Then she waited and felt glad that the pleasure of her friends' imminent arrival outbalanced her faint intimations of danger.

Where Sebalrai had gone and almost driven herself insane, Skjebne followed cautiously. Kell comforted the girl and stroked her hair, whispering constantly that all she had seen was illusion. Hora brought water and a slightly narcotic liquor that the wyrda used for the pain of wounds in battle: just a few drops were enough to soothe her into a drowse.

'Most likely she will soon drift into a natural sleep,' Hora said. She was a small and fragile thing in this state, limp as a doll with a simple, innocent prettiness that allowed the man to understand the strength of Kell's feelings for her.

'I don't know what happened.' Kell pointed to the Guardian Helmet that Skjebne held in his hands. 'She was curious about it, then I saw her lower it over her head . . . Is there a poison inside? Some kind of defence to warn the uninitiated away?'

'Maybe it was intended for the wyrda alone.'

'You may be right Skjebne.' Thorbyorg stood at the threshold of the crystal room. 'Though why that should be so remains a mystery to me. I have donned the helmet oftentimes and noted nothing unusual in the wearing.'

'Well, First Eolder, this is a puzzle we are under some pressure to solve. Either you or I must try the helmet again – not forgetting all that has happened in recent days.'

'You think the helmet has changed?'

Skjebne's grin was broad and provocative. 'I think it has

been activated, Thorbyorg. I think events are moving on apace and the helmet, or whatever controls it, has recognised that fact.'

And so saying, and noticing the new reticence in the old fighter's eyes, Skjebne lowered it over his head.

For some seconds there was no reaction whatever, and the silence grew intense within the room. Then, to the onlookers' astonishment, Skjebne started to laugh; and when he spoke it was with an unnatural clarity, as though the air itself were generating the words inside the listeners' ears.

'So . . . that is how it has been . . .'

'Can you see anything?' Kell was curious to know.

'Yes, wonderful things. Have you ever considered, Thorbyorg, why the Guardian Helmet is so called?'

'Well, we supposed it was guarding the secrets of the Rad in some way. Or maybe the head of the wearer,' he added lamely, taking two shots at the target.

'Both of those, and much more besides. There are understandings here beyond anything I had ever imagined; secrets, yes – but only until the time was right for their revelation. Thorbyorg, I know where your people have travelled in *Heavenwalker* and *Cloudfarer*. Wrynn, I have gained crucial insights into the Thrall Makers' work and know why that work must now cease. Hora, I can direct the whole hierarchy of orbs wherever I happen to be, as long as I'm wearing the helmet. And Kell . . .'

Skjebne removed the Guardian Helmet and there was both sadness and excitement in his eyes.

'. . . I have seen the face of the All Mother, and now I know her name.'

★

Presently the light in the dell weakened a little although the shadows did not lengthen at all. Wherever the sun might be in the sky, its rays did not simply penetrate the mists around Kairos. Rather, it seemed as though the vapours took up the light and gathered it into a hoard and used it adaptably, for maximum effect. And so the essence of the city decided when darkness would fall and – so Feoh's experience had been – chose those nights that were clear and filled with stars. Similarly storms were unknown here, because in the time of blizzards and the hard-long-dark the frugal haze gave out its stores of sunshine to warm Kairos and the surrounding hills.

Now, for whatever mysterious reason, Feoh was being treated to a mellow evening time. The mists were thin and delicate and laced with a subtle perfume. The air became stilled. And out of that stillness a forewarning grew.

Feoh roused herself, swept up the hacele and wrapped it about her body. She drew her knife from its scabbard and slipped behind the apple tree to be hidden from the rock spires that had suddenly become more significant.

She noticed that the centre of the calm lay between two particular columns. The mist was heavier there and the light was increasing. Presently she heard voices coming closer, and made herself ready.

'But it can't be so simple! You have just led us into a different room . . .'

'In all my years living here I had never suspected these byways . . .'

'They exist by the same means that draws the Great Orbs to other places in a twinkling. The pathways link here and there without crossing the distance between . . .'

'But where are we? Oh, some kind of woodland –'

Kell emerged first, with the silver-grey wulf Fenrir close behind.

The shadow slipped from behind the tree without warning and was upon him. Even Fenrir had no time to react as Feoh, to the boy's acute embarrassment, hugged him close towards her and kissed him firmly on the cheek.

8

The Shining Ones

It was shocking enough for Kell to be so affectionately greeted: Hora suffered more because he knew what was coming. Skjebne accepted Feoh's welcome with a rare tolerance, and Sebalrai used the opportunity to compliment Feoh on her appearance, and in particular the gorgeous moonstone she wore at her brow.

'Well, when it is time I will give you one that is just the same,' Feoh said. *Yes, that much is clear*, she thought, *but there is also so much darkness*. She realised how far her own abilities had matured; and in seeing Kell and Sebalrai together she knew now that only death would separate them.

The others thought her quietness was due to Wrynn's presence. Feoh smiled at the mage a little shyly, and in their glance acknowledged that they would save what had to be said between themselves until later.

'Let us return to the city,' Wrynn advised, 'and make our plans there. Kairos itself already knows I am back, but I would keep my arrival secret from the Brothers as long as possible. Here too gossip moves faster than any man can run.'

So they made their way, with Feoh commenting how nimbly Skjebne was walking.

'Wrynn has given me a rare gift,' he replied, and went on to tell of the Radiant Iron and explain some of the events that had unfolded since they were last together.

A short time later a tall and imposing woman in a striking blue robe walked along the white-walled alley to her home. She needed to stoop to avoid the doorway's low lintel, and left the door open a few moments before closing it to the world. Feoh the Healer she was called on the streets; Sustren some *feolc* said, and it was probably true to judge by the way the air lensed oddly around her as she moved, and how the rippling preceded the sound of soft voices from within her apartment, as though she was speaking in tongues . . .

'It is exhausting,' Sebalrai gasped. 'I can't −' And her concentration slipped and her friends became visible again. Skjebne was delighted.

'I have never seen you maintain the spell so completely for so long, or shield so many. Well done.'

'I think we have avoided prying eyes,' Wrynn said. 'Besides, you will be lodging elsewhere. And soon enough it will not matter anyway because by then we will have moved on to Arcanum.'

'The abode of the All Mother, where Shamra has been taken.'

'Yes.' Wrynn nodded. 'But we must be sure of our forces and the means of our approach, Skjebne. None of us has been to Arcanum before. It will certainly be very well protected. Although we have the powerful wyrda to fight on our behalf, and although your wulfen friends, Kell, have promised their allegiance, sheer strength and weaponry might not be the most effective means of attack.'

'We also have the orbs,' Skjebne reminded them. '*Sky-*

master and *Windhover* and the travel orbs – and now through the revelations of the Guardian Helmet a knowledge of the byways of the Rad.'

'Yes, yes. Breaching Arcanum's defences might be a simple matter of *appearing there*, just as we entered Kairos. But we don't know that. We also don't know how far the Thrall Brothers will support us in our aim. Many of them are beguiled by the Sustren – yes, as I am,' the mage added to forestall Skjebne's obvious response. 'But the Sisters are true to the Goddess, whereas Feoh is not.'

'And never will be after the pain she has brought to my friends and myself.'

Wrynn went on. 'There is one friend I think we can trust – the mage Orael. He is *lyblaeca*, powerful in his thrall-making, and he has never trusted the Sustren or fallen prey to their wiles, being staunchly outspoken against them and the incursions of the Goddess into our culture. His quarters lie up in the hills within the walls of the sanctum. He will meet with us I'm sure and give his good advice. I will arrange for us to see him tomorrow.'

'But that will do for today,' Feoh said. She had noticed how Wrynn's apprehension was fixed in the future, spoiling the peace of the present moment. 'Now we will eat a supper together, and drink *meodu*, and then share the adventures we've had since our last meeting. I daresay you've encountered some interesting folk on the way?'

'Oh indeed,' Kell piped up, suddenly remembering. He grinned broadly and reached inside his tunic. 'In fact I have brought one of them with me. His name is Tsep.'

They talked long into what passed for the night in Kairos. For a lengthy span the sky turned a glorious purple streaked with amber cloud. Closer to the horizon, the world was rimmed with green. After Skjebne's casual comment about this as he peered through the window, Feoh took her guests outside to a small private courtyard largely shaded by a lyre tree whose tautly strung seed filaments hummed and whispered in the gentlest breeze.

'The feldlands beyond the city will be much colder than this, of course,' Feoh explained. 'The mists provide an effective barrier against the elements. It never snows here, and any frosts are delicate and fleeting. Sometimes we see the sun – sometimes it shines clear and bright from a sky of natural blue. But most often Kairos is winged by an ambient light filled with these beautiful displays.'

'Who chooses?' Skjebne asked, innocently enough it seemed. 'I mean, do you suppose there is an intelligence guiding the sky's appearance?' He was thinking of weorthan. He was thinking of Perth and the way the sun shone there under the All Mother's rule.

'Kairos is incredibly ancient,' Wrynn answered. 'And it has been the Thrall Makers' home for the most of that time. Nothing in our literature speaks of any controlling presence beyond the Brothers themselves. We have never found ourselves under the sway of the Goddess until the Sustren arrived. My own feeling is that the shields around Kairos are mindless, but sensitive to the wider world, and maybe to the mood of the people. Do you not think that the Makers of the Thrall would *know* they were being enchanted?'

'But that is the very essence of delusion,' Skjebne replied, smiling as graciously as Wrynn had done. 'It is always invisible.' Nevertheless he accepted the mage's point and said no more about it. The conversation waned.

In the quiet yard the company sipped their honeyed liquor, and Fenrir dozed beneath the lyre tree dreaming of the endless forest, while Tsep flickered among the branches catching moths. As his wings clipped the strung seedthreads the air thrummed softly with musical notes.

'It is wonderfully peaceful here,' Kell said, smelling the perfume of the night. The sky was so gorgeously violet and dark, dark blue beyond the moving mist that trembled with such fragile, shifting colours.

'It is how all the world should be,' Hora spoke up unexpectedly. The meodu had mellowed him so he did not feel angry. Rather, the others detected a sorrow behind his words.

'What sadness there is in the fact that men and women have battled the Ice for so long, only to have survived to war with each other now!'

'Well said *brooor*.' Skjebne smiled at his dear friend. 'But having given this question much thought, I am bound to say that the very instinct for survival causes men to fight. Rage is what keeps the heart beating –'

'There must be more to it than that,' Feoh said. 'The Seetus survives and it does not fight. Faras and the Shore Folk live in a similar way, at peace with themselves and the world. And look here, the Thrall Makers have existed in tranquillity for countless spans of time.'

'Well . . .' Skjebne nodded and sipped from his cup. 'Notice little Tsep who pitches his skill against those insects. And Fenrir slumbers now, and dreams of the kill. And if the drengs of Helcyrian were to come over that wall, wouldn't we all snatch up some weapon and slaughter as many as necessary to preserve our own lives?'

'This must be deeper than the Goddess,' commented

Sebalrai. 'She could not have put these forces inside us, because we are using them now to oppose her.'

'I agree. Earlier, when I first wore the Guardian Helmet, I was offered wisdoms in such profusion that the experience almost overwhelmed me – as it did you, *sweor*. For a little while I could make no sense of it, but then I started to understand.'

Skjebne glanced at his other friends, Kell and Hora and Feoh. 'Do you remember, as we were planning to leave Perth, we came upon what you called a place of stories, Feoh? There we found thousands of crystal discs – and Kell, you discovered learnings in the jewel. We took some away with us in the ice wain, but circumstance prevented us from exploring them.'

'I remember. I saw a dark-skinned, noble people. I saw an image of the true sun dazzling in the sky!'

'Yes, yes. Well imagine the contents of all of those discs gathered up into one hoard. That is what I found within the Guardian Helmet. And more. Imagine a teacher present also, but one wiser and nobler than any in the Tutorium. He – or she, for you may choose – can guide you through that wealth of learnings, leading or following your curiosity as it explores. And imagine too that with a tilt of your attention the lesson can be put aside, and you can use the helmet to look through the eyes of any orb that exists, and direct one or all of them with a silent, instant command.

'That tells you something of the Guardian Helmet's power. And through its instruction I came to know more of the All Mother . . .

'When the Ice first threatened the world, before the globe was engulfed, men created the Goddess to oversee the efforts of all of Humanity to survive. Before that happened the entire population, many millions upon millions of souls, busied themselves in some way or other and employed a huge variety of *ferhocraeft*, what the Guardian Helmet has called teknology. A powerful guild of wrights built the Orbs and the Universal Wheel to guide them. Other mages of incredible skill – the precursors of the Makers of the Thrall – wove life's fabrics into the wulfen and the Hreaomus, the Seetus, the Auroks and many other breeds. Vast mechanisms carved out the enclaves like Perth where communities could live in some kind of safety. The industry of the human kin was boundless, and all of it at first was directed by an esoteric engine that mimicked the operations of a man's brain. But just as you, Wrynn, have said that the controlling force behind Kairos is mindless, so it proved to be with the device that guided the huge preparations for the Wintering. There was intelligence without insight; knowledge without understanding. And so the creators of the engine determined that their scheme would work only if they infused the dead metals with human warmth, a living soul whose decisions would be made with the very instincts of which we have spoken.

'The Brothers of the Thrall were instructed to carry out the necessary operations to incorporate the *onweardnes* of an individual into a weorthan matrix – or something like weorthan, for rigid crystal has its limitations. And the chosen one was a woman, and her name was Kvasir.'

Here Skjebne paused and his eyes took on a wistful cast, as though across his heart blew the winds of many emotions that he had no wish to express.

'I have tried to imagine how she must have felt, knowing

that she was giving herself up to eternity. Within the shining confines of her domain, she would look on as her friends grew old and perished, and their children and their children all down the ages turned to dust. With a warm heart and with bright and brooding wings she must nurture the communities in her care and preserve in them, as much as in herself, the dream of the future after the Ice had gone.

'Well, such was the plan. But you know that in its wisdom and its kindness Wierd grants us a limited span. We are made to appreciate horizons. Our very mortality gives life its sweetness and vigour. What could immortality really bring except madness? And that is just what happened. As the generations passed and were ploughed under, and as the Ice intensified its grip, alone in her glittering prison Kvasir the All Mother slowly became insane. Oh, she still carried life's first imperative within her – to breathe, eat, play, love, sing – but more and more she wanted these things for herself. And who,' said Skjebne, lifting his *meodu* cup high, 'could blame her?'

'And is that why she established the Sustren, to exact some sort of revenge?' asked Wrynn.

'Well, my feeling is that the Sisters were sent out into the world because the Goddess herself is trapped. Oh she – or at least elements of her fractured personality – exist within every weorthan matrix in the world. Even the smallest nuggets will contain something of her influence, which is why weorthan has proved so dangerous for us.'

And so saying, Skjebne reached into his pocket and produced a lump of the crystal; a white oval pebble, smoothed and battered as though by the sea – except at one end, which had been finely cut to offer a window into the gem. Skjebne first passed the crystal to Hora, who gazed into the clear depths of the stone before his eyes lost their focus, and then became moist.

'By the Rad, Skjebne. What Fenrir witnessed in Perth, then, was true . . .'

'It makes sense of a great deal that has happened. Hand the nugget on, Hora.'

One by one each person there in the twilit courtyard stared into the glass, even Tsep whose nosiness overcame his hunger for insects. He flittered down on to Kell's shoulder as the boy raised the weorthan to the man-bat's eyes.

'How did you come by it, Skjebne?'

'There is weorthan aboard all the great orbs, I am sure. Some of it is neutral, empty of imagery. But the Guardian Helmet can impress any of the knowledge it contains directly into the glass. Once it revealed Kvasir's original face, I asked it to duplicate the image.'

'She looks more like Shamra than Fenrir made out.' Kell was the last to look upon the stone, and did so for a long span before returning it to Skjebne. 'But Shamra grown into womanhood.'

'She is beautiful,' offered Sebalrai, with as much generosity as she could muster.

'Any girl who is born with this likeness becomes the focus of the All Mother's special attention. One can imagine that every so often Wierd produces a child who reminds Kvasir of herself – of her living, human self. And then, most cruelly, the All Mother's torture is repeated and intensified as she watches the child flourish and age and wither away. In her desperation Kvasir has gone to extreme lengths to safeguard her simulacrum – remember in Thule, the woman who was half dreng, her flesh preserved by metal and the force of ligetu.'

'Then Shamra was born,' added Feoh. 'And just before she attained womanhood we took her away from Perth, out of the All Mother's reach.'

Skjebne nodded. 'Her fury must have been endless, and yet as nothing compared to her frustration. By that point, some ten seasons ago, the Sustren had discovered Kairos and realised the importance of the Thrall Brothers, the direct descendants of those who had created the All Mother during the onset of the Ice. Could it be that they had the *ferhocraeft* to uncreate what their forefathers had made? Could they possibly lift the soul of Kvasir from her crystal cell and replace it within Shamra's flesh?'

'That is a question that perhaps you can answer, Wrynn,' Feoh said.

The mage's expression was dark.

'My fear is that the *lyblaeca* can do exactly that. Orael and a few of the others among the master enchanters have spoken of the extent of their powers at Gebedraedan. I suspect they have been compelled to keep their silence through threats or promises – the Sisters are capable of both. Indeed, it was the hints that Orael gave as much as meeting Feoh that prompted me to seek you, Skjebne, and do something about the situation before it got out of hand.'

'So we will do something.' Skjebne conjured a smile and tilted back his head. The sky over Kairos was now as dark as it would get, and on a trickster whim the mists had magnified the stars so they hung like ghostly globes above the city, twinkling faintly green, gold, blue . . . 'It is late on. I suggest we take some rest. And early tomorrow, Wrynn, you will send for us?'

'Yes, we'll meet Orael at the day's beginning. I'll take you to a lodging now – though I suggest that Sebalrai and perhaps Fenrir remain here; so she and Feoh will be well protected, and in instant contact with you.'

'Good enough.' Skjebne rose, stretching the stiffness out of his limbs. 'Let's go now. The *meodou* has wearied me more than one of Hora's fishing stories . . .'

He stirred himself to leave and the others followed suit. But Feoh hung back as Skjebne led the way into the house and caught Kell's attention by a gentle touch on his arm.

'Alderamin gave me this a long time ago. I have kept it with me, letting it bide its time. And now I pass it to you to use as you wish.'

She held a heorotskin pouch, and now loosened the drawstring and dropped a faceted blue stone into Kell's hand. It was half the size of his fist, a beautiful and precious thing.

'I remember this. Alderamin offered us each a gift in gratitude.'

She nodded. 'He told me this jewel contains a power like the sun, and that its soul will know when that force is to be unleashed. I feel the time is near.'

'But –'

'Don't fear it Kell, it will not destroy you. You too will realise when the moment comes to release the light of Wierd.'

Wrynn's judgement was sound in choosing a lodge – a 'fleeting house' it was locally called – that was modest and anonymous and tucked away in a backwater street where comings and goings were not so likely noticed. Although the mage had paid for three rooms, Skjebne, Hora and Kell (with Tsep nestled close) stayed in one, for safety's sake. Each took a turn in remaining awake while the other two slept, for there could be no denying the faintly sinister *onweardnes* that Kairos seemed to possess, like a distant music that only now and then comes to one's notice.

It happened that after some hours the quality of the light outside changed. The subtly textured blues and violets ebbed from the sky, which filled with a stronger, brassier light. It was day's beginning, as the Thrall Maker had called it (Wrynn never referred to it as dawn). Shortly afterwards, as the three were tucking into cornbread and waterfruit and fine ripe cheese, with Tsep nosing in corners for spiders, there came a gentle knocking at the door.

Immediately a dagger appeared in Hora's hand and Tsep flew to a niche above the lintel, ready to act in the event of ambush. Skjebne calmed his friends with a gesture.

'Who are you?'

'Dweorg of the Brising,' came a gruff but friendly voice.

'And who sent you?'

'The mage named Wrynn. I am to take you to a meeting with the Thrall Brother Orael . . . Wait, I have a note of confirmation.'

A brief scuffling of cloth or paper followed, and then a square of yellow parchment was pushed beneath the door. A number of marks had been made upon it; words and sigils, some of them obviously wyrda. Kell shook his head.

'What use is this? None of us can decipher these characters — and the images of the Craeftum might be a simple deception.'

I suppose you need to be suspicious, given you have so few useful senses!

Tsep dropped lightly down from his ledge and touched his nose to the parchment.

Wrynn wrote this undoubtedly. He was even-tempered as he

did so. Feoh was in the room with him at this time and — sniff
sniff — *Fenrir also. The wulf had just broken his fast on some
salted heorot meat, not of the best quality I'm bound to say . . .*

Kell laughed aloud at his friend's antics, while full of
admiration for his amazing capability. He relayed Tsep's
impressions to Skjebne, whose smile of appreciation was as
broad as the boy's.

'Enter Dweorg of the Brising, and welcome!'

The old ironwood door flew aside and there stood a man
who was stockier than Hora but barely half Kell's height.
The gnome's shoulders and barrel chest were protected by
chunkily wrought iron plate skimmed with a dusting of
rust, but his lower arms and thick muscular legs were bare.
He wore stoutly made but well-worn leather boots cross-
laced to the top of his shins, which were similarly shielded
by iron. He held a pair of battered leather work gloves
which he waved in greeting to these strangers. His smile
seemed genuine and was oddly endearing, given his
squarish crookedly rooted teeth and the broad gaps
between them. Dweorg gave off the smell of coal and
steel and sulphur as he waited there with his fists jammed
on his hips.

'So, will we go now? I have much work to do this day!'

The dwarf led the company by an intricate route
through the puzzle of streets, to an even poorer quarter of
shanties where others of Dweorg's kind were living. Once
or twice they caught sight of lone women, each one dark
and tall and elegant in her bearing. They were clearly
Sustren. Kell looked while trying not to seem too curious.
A first glance tempted him to think that there was nothing
special about them, but then each time his deeper senses
recognised their uniqueness and he understood in a distant

way how the Thrall Brothers had come to fall under their spell.

With an effort Kell brought his attention back to the immediate surroundings. He was reminded of the earth-workers' settlements in the hills around Thule, and it came to him that these folk, the Brising, were another link in that chain, working the metals that had been wrenched else-where from the ground.

And so it proved to be as the boy spoke with Dweorg, while Hora kept a sharp eye open for danger.

'Aye, your guesses are shrewd, youth,' Dweorg said, making Kell smile since the dwarf constantly interrupted his conversation by waving and calling greetings to friends as they passed by. 'The Brising have mined the land and worked its fruit for many generations, bringing the earths and metals we find in the Firenful Hills here to Kairos.'

'Firenful Hills?'

'The Wicked Hills, boy. There are creatures who live in the soil that can take your leg off with a single bite. They come and hunt the Brising like an Ice bear roots for grubs among the stones.'

'What – do they look like?'

'Oh ho! The *snaka* chew through the ground as fast as you can run. They don't have eyeballs, but writhing clusters of red tentacles in their sockets instead. Their skin is pebbly and dark, so that they can lie curled in a pocket in the earth, or on the surface among rocks, so cleverly that you don't see them at all – until you stand on one and realise to your horror that you are being eaten alive!'

Tsep chortled at this tale, though it concerned him slightly that Kell seemed to swallow it whole without chewing, such was the power of conviction that the little yarnspinner possessed.

'Oh, I see. Well I wouldn't like to walk in the Firenful Hills, that's for sure . . . and why Brising? What does that name mean, Dweorg?'

'We are the Shining Ones,' the dwarf announced with some pride. 'Though we are dark of cast, and labour in shadowy places, we are master metalwrights and produce tools and weapons that glitter and gleam as the outcome of our craft. Also, despite the mean way in which we have been forged, our hearts shine like the sun for our love of life!'

'What do you mean "forged"?'

'Why, we too were bent to this shape. Is it not common practice in your land? In a time beyond memory the Thrall Makers came down into Kairos and took people from the streets, and through the great ritual of *Gebedraedan* changed the filaments of meaning that existed inside them. And the children of those first-chosen became the Brising; small and broad, strong of sinew and soul. And now we thank the *lyblaeca* for the gift of our identity.'

Dweorg was still grinning at the glory of his tale, but Kell was appalled.

Do you hear this, Tsep. These people allowed the mages to change them!

No more than Wrynn changed you and Skjebne and Sebalrai with the favour of Radiant Iron. Look at Dweorg, not at yourself. He and his kin are happy to be as they are. Besides, the first-chosen might well have agreed to the ritual of the Thrall.

But −

Remember what Skjebne told us earlier, that the ancient Thrall Brothers created the Seetus, the wulfen, my kin the Hraeomus and

138

others . . . Kell, don't you suppose that such interventions
allowed life to continue through the Ice?

Even so, it is an evil thing to succumb to such an outrage!

Ah well, it is done. And there can be no giving back.

By and by they noticed that the air was astir: a constant
breeze poured past them towards a towering compound of
buildings, out of which came shouts and hammerings and
intermittent flashes of blue fire.

'These are the foundries where the Brising practise their
craft,' Dweorg explained, lifting his voice a little above the
increasing din.

'There are fires but no smokes,' Skjebne pointed out.
Dweorg nodded and smiled at the thin man's keen-eyed
cleverness.

'The fumes are drawn down through ducts deep in the
ground, and vented out far across the feldlands. That is why
you feel the streaming breezes now – they take away the
stinks.' The dwarf tapped the side of his nose and grimaced.
'The Thrall Makers for all their influence, and the *spedigfeolc*
– the wealthy ones – have such delicate nostrils!'

He gave a great bellowing laugh, which was lost among
the rising clatter and clangings from the great forging halls.
The party entered and as their eyes grew used to the flaring
light and sudden shadows, they made out other Brising
workers labouring alone, in pairs, in larger gangs. Now and
then the mighty bulking form of a mox-like creature was to
be seen, hauling ore or loads of finished goods; but the
dwarves also seemed to make use of the kind of unseen
fields that Kell had experienced in Hugauga, for rods and
spheres and strips of yellow semi-liquid metal went gliding
by in the distance without visible support.

'Orael wants to meet us here?' Skjebne wondered. He

could barely hear himself think. Dweorg shrugged and his iron shoulderpads heaved up.

'Neutral ground. Besides, none of the Sustren is likely to come here. There are quieter chambers though. I will take you to your rendezvous.'

The dwarf pointed off to the right and the company cut down between tall stacks of sheet steel. As they came to an intersection another of the Brising, one even stouter than Dweorg, with oil-blackened skin and wide white eyes went scurrying past. He was shouting something that the others failed to catch –

But Tsep, nuzzled down in Kell's tunic, was alerted to the sudden flash of fear in the man. He hurled an impression all-at-once into Kell's mind –

And the boy grabbed Dweorg by the scruff of his neck as he reached the end of the alley, and dragged him back clear of the rolls of steel cable, which at that instant went tumbling by.

Skjebne yelled in shock and Hora put a steadying hand on his shoulder. Dweorg had stumbled backwards and sat upon the ground. Now he scrambled up panting, glanced at the cable drums and then up at Kell.

'Beorn, you have saved my life!'

'Well, actually, Tsep –'

Dweorg grabbed Kell's hand and shook it vigorously in a knuckle-cracking grip.

'Tsep, yes, whoever . . . such accidents as these sometimes happen, and I am usually prepared for them . . . but today being different, and my pondering over Orael . . . I can only thank you.'

'There's really no need.'

Then the light in the Brising's eyes altered. Kell noticed

that the spun rings in those eyes was a translucent orange, the colour of the fires that Dweorg faced every day.

'No,' the dwarf said, 'I can do more. Listen my friends, for later I will deny that I told you this. Wrynn made arrangements with me late last night. We have known one another a very long time, and our mutual trust is well founded. He paid me money to take you into the hills, to the Thrall Makers' sanctum, there to meet Orael.

'But after that, as I was reaching the end of my work time here, Orael himself appeared and gave me more gold and different instructions. Now I was to bring you here to the foundry at the time of the beginning-light. I was to leave you in the room that he appointed, and go to my work and say nothing of my errand.'

Dweorg's lips curled in a sneer. 'I know we are taught to respect the *lyblaeca*. But he did not seem right to my eye, and I did not trust him. I have no solid reason to believe so, but I think the man is a betrayer.'

'There, the words are out.' So saying Dweorg reached into the money-pouch at his belt and snatched out a small bag of coin and hurled it away.

'Now I am in debt to no one. But if any of you need my assistance at any future time, just come and find Dweorg of the Brising, and he will be willing to help you.'

The dwarf shook Kell's hand again even harder, and bowed to Hora and Skjebne. Then he pointed out a route through the alleys of steel to a black doorway beyond; bowed again and scuttled out of sight.

'So.' Skjebne looked at his friends and considered their faces, as though their very expressions could help him decide. 'Do we go ahead with our rendezvous?'

'What of Wrynn?' was Hora's point. 'Does this mean he has betrayed us as well?'

'Tsep told us that when Wrynn wrote his letter he was even-tempered –'

I would have detected treachery by the smell on the vellum, Kell, Tsep added.

'He is a mage, he might easily have enchanted us,' was Hora's view.

'But why take all that trouble in Hugauga? Why not simply have tempted us here to the Thrall Makers' stronghold in the first place?'

'We could spend the rest of the day playing this game,' Skjebne declared. 'Should we walk away now, then if Wrynn has deceived us we will find Feoh's home empty and our business will take us into the hills – as it will do anyway if we meet with Orael and find him true of heart. All routes lead to the sanctum of the *lyblaeca*.'

So saying, Skjebne checked the weapons he was carrying and encouraged the others to do the same. Then they took the path that Dweorg had indicated until they came to the door at the end.

'Enter and be welcome,' said a resonant voice within at Skjebne's tentative tap. Kell heard the creak of leather behind him as Hora tensed himself for the attack . . .

But it never came. Skjebne opened the door and stepped inside, and there they were greeted by Orael the mage who was, if this were possible, even taller and more regally imposing than Wrynn. The man's robes were of the deepest purple, the same dark shade as Kairos' evening sky, tantalising the eye into thinking they were black. And Kell's initial comparison seemed even more apt as Orael moved forward and the material swung and swirled with tiny glimmerings; diamond dust, the illusion of stars.

'I must thank you for tolerating my suspicious nature,' said the mage. He was long of face and his eyes were cool and unsympathetic. His skin showed an unusual gloss and bore the wrinkles of great age, and yet his movement and manner were those of a much younger man.

'The involvement of the Sustren in the *lyblaeca's* affairs has reached a new level. The sanctum is not the best place to discuss our business, since even in an empty chamber many spies might be listening.' He gave a brief and cheerless smile, and indicated a rough table at the other end of the room with chairs around and a simple offering of refreshment.

'May I suggest that we agree our plans here now, deciding on the best way of preventing the Sustren from corrupting the purpose of the Thrall in giving the Goddess life in the flesh . . .'

'Sound sense.' Skjebne beamed amiably and motioned for Hora to go ahead, making sure that he was ahead of Orael as Skjebne moved in front of Kell, then stumbled unexpectedly as though his leg was weakened.

'Oh – forgive me. An old wound . . .'

The mage made no move to assist, but Skjebne gripped his arm for support, bringing his other hand round to clench Orael's palm in thanks – and made a swift brief movement then held the hand up for all to see.

The fleen that Skjebne had taken from Feoh's apartment had cut deep, parting the flesh in a long grey gash, out of which not a drop of blood had spilled.

9

Place Of The Thrall

'Use the Radiant Iron to heal yourself, mage,' Skjebne said, very quietly.

'The balm does not work instantly . . .' Orael made a feeble attempt at defence, but then abandoned it and laughed – a laugh that turned into a snarl and then into a high-pitched howl which penetrated the head like needles.

Skjebne used the fleen a second time, ripping up through the mage's robe and the flesh beneath.

'He's not alive!' Kell stared upon the laceration in horror, taking a second to notice the way the grey flaps of skin had curled apart, and the glint of a black, tarry substance within – but only a second, for then Hora acted; hauling Orael backwards and slamming him down to the floor, then dropped his entire huge weight on to the Thrall Maker's neck.

The bones snapped with a loud crack and the mage began thrashing about amongst the crude chairs, toppling the table and scattering its arrangement of cups.

'He's not dead, either,' Hora said wryly. Though Orael was surely disabled. The penetrating whining note faded and his strugglings started to lessen.

'He is not likely to have come alone.' Skjebne dropped

the fleen and snatched a fire weapon from its sheath hidden under his tunic. Hora withdrew a short stabbing sword. Kell took hold of his knife.

'We must get away from here –'

'And go to Feoh's house,' Hora added. 'She and Wrynn will know what to do!'

Skjebne remained silent, but Kell noticed his expression and wondered also if they would ever see Feoh again.

They moved to the door, then slipped out into the noise and gloom of the foundry floor. Although they saw no one approaching along the alley of metal stacks, Skjebne chose another way that skirted the room and led them by a more direct route to the great hangar doors and outside.

Kell – Kell! Tsep was calling. *Let me fly ahead and check for danger.*

Kell did so, releasing the hreaomus who went flittering away into the cavernous shadows.

'I think he was Slean,' Hora said, thinking of Orael, as the three negotiated their way between the stacked metal as cautiously yet as quickly as they could. The warrior was thinking of the time a similar creature had been destroyed on the night when Shamra was taken. Then the forces of its own ship departing had ended its life, or whatever force animated the thing. Like Orael, the Slean soldier had once been a man, but grotesquely transformed. Perhaps this too was the work of the *lyblaeca*, trying to weave the magics of Wierd without understanding its nature . . . But however it had been, Hora recalled that where you found Slean you also found –

Kell! Kell!

Tsep came spinning back out of the dark, its eyes alight with agitation.

145

There are the machine insects just up ahead. They are responding to Orael's call!

Sure enough, the dimness was astir with movement and the crinkling sounds of the creatures unfolding their limbs. A claw squeaked on sheet steel. Something scuttered across the top of a stack and dropped down into the passageway, hissing amidst its tangle of legs.

Skjebne discharged the fire weapon and by the flash of light and the ball of sparks that erupted just beside it, the group caught sight of their enemy – one of the *hyrnetu* that had ambushed them in Hugauga.

Get away little brooor, Kell called to Tsep's mind as the man-bat swept about in circles just overhead. But Tsep even in his fear would not be drawn by cowardice into the abandonment of his friends.

Two more hyrnetu appeared over the piles of metal ahead. One joined its companion, effectively blocking the way; the other ran with its unnerving many-legged gait across the top. And behind the trapped company, there came a bristling as several others worked their way around, so perfecting the trap.

Hora turned his back to Kell and strained to see in the darkness. Yes – there was movement; the slide of light on a spidery limb; and that same vicious hissing sound by which the hyrnetu hoped to terrorise their prey. And yes, they were growing more visible now, their surfaces glowing as the air itself seemed to brighten . . .

'Skjebne!' Hora gave a warning cry, but there was no outrunning the stream of molten metal that shot high in an arc above the stacks of steel sheet and poured down over the insects. They were instantly enveloped, stopped in their tracks, engulfed by liquid iron. One exploded, showering globules of flame all around, one of which skimmed Hora's face and left a raw burn weal in its wake.

Skjebne fired again and again into the two hyrnetu blocking the way, and loosed a pulse of energy at the third creature looming above. It jolted, writhed, and was whisked away all in an instant. Dweorg appeared in its place with a fierce grin stamped on his face.

'It was fortunate, I think, that I let my distrust of the mage get the better of me!'

Even as he spoke his fellow Brisings were attacking the two remaining hyrnetu blocking the alley ahead: some boldly ran up to the insects and entangled them in nets, while others jabbed with a kind of powerful ligetu prod that sparked and crackled at the tip, and delivered a paralysing jolt.

Within seconds the machine insects had been laid low, and the crisis was over. The mangled hyrnetu were dragged clear and the company walked towards the light, stopping close to the great outer doors where Dweorg soon joined them.

'We are indebted to you twice,' Skjebne said with a note of deep gratitude; and the dwarf smiled not so much at the compliment, but in the knowledge that his instincts about Orael had proved sound.

'Acts of friendship are nothing like currency, and so no payment is due. I think the lyblaeca will thank us for revealing the extent to which the Sustren have corrupted their guild.' Then his smile faded as he thought of what had been done to the mage. 'Have you any knowledge of what Orael became? I saw him briefly as you hurried from the room . . .'

'I can offer only guesswork, and sparsely at that.' Skjebne

recounted the incident near Faras's village. 'Whether the warrior was alive or just animated in some way, like the hyrnetu, I still cannot say. Perhaps Orael was conscious of his transformation; maybe he had even desired it –'

Dweorg shrugged. 'Maybe so. Perhaps the enchanter himself was enthralled by Sustren glamour. He was not a young man; and if he had lengthy work yet to be completed he may have wanted to extend his life in this way . . .'

'That's an interesting speculation, although I wonder if it was Orael at all – possibly the Slean was a likeness of the living individual.' He was thinking of the other *lyblaeca*, and then of the lesser Brothers, like Wrynn. If they had been similarly tainted then this mission to Kairos was a hundred times more dangerous.

'I will be interested to know the outcome –' Dweorg paused as two of his kind hurried over and handed him something wrapped loosely in cloth.

'You will go to the sanctum now?' he said.

Skjebne nodded. 'After we have returned to Feoh's home. We have to know what has happened to our friends.'

'Aye, well may Wierd guide your way to good fortune. Avoid the Sustren as best you can – your little winged *gefera* will smell them out. And when you meet the Makers of the Thrall, give them this.'

He unfolded the cloth and showed them a finger still wearing Orael's ring.

'The token will get you through the gates. It is the mage's unique and personal jewel and would have been of great value to him – while he was still a man.'

Shortly afterwards they made their farewells and Skjebne,

following Dweorg's detailed instructions, led his friends through the backstreets of the town towards Feoh's dwelling place. Although the day was bright (compelling Tsep to huddle tight in Kell's tunic) and the cityzens went about their business with good cheer, Skjebne and Hora and Kell felt a gathering gloom as they came to the narrow street which was familiar to them, and then to Feoh's door with its black iron ringbolt and latch. It was unlocked and lifted without hindrance. The men went inside.

'Empty,' Kell said heavily, even before Skjebne had checked the sleeping room and Hora the little courtyard at the back. Then he felt Tsep moving and opened his tunic to let the man-bat go free.

I smell the story that was told here, Kell, and the place is not deserted.

Tsep leaped from the chairback where he was perched and disappeared under the table; fluttered about there briefly and shot back into view.

Here! A hatch cover — a space beneath. But there is blood —

Kell pushed the table aside and snatched away a straw *healm* that half covered the hatch Tsep had detected. Blood was indeed smeared on the boards and around the iron ring that Kell now used to haul the cover free.

Underneath was a small bolt hole, half a man's height and barely long or wide enough for him to stretch his limbs. A smell of damp rose up to Kell's nostrils as he peered into the darkness.

'Here! Over here!'

Skjebne came quickly to the call, and moments later Hora clumped across with a lit candle, dropped to his knees and moved the light this way and that.

'Empty. They are all gone from here . . .'

No – no!

Kell reached down into the hole, troubled by Tsep's insistence – and snatched his hand away again with a yell.

'I felt something.'

Kell, this is wulfen blood. I smell the living wulf, and –

'Sebalrai. Sebalrai, we're here. You're safe now. We're here . . .'

And gradually as the girl emerged from her fear so she came into view, her blood-streaked arms wrapped about Fenrir, whose eyes were closed and whose tongue was lolling from his jaws. He was barely breathing.

'Feoh – s-said the Sisters were coming . . .' A single tear rolled down Sebalrai's cheek. 'She put me in here and told me to hide – she – said I was not to come out until you returned – she . . .'

'You can come out of there now child,' Skjebne said gently. 'We can attend to you better then, and to Fenrir too.'

Hora lifted the girl out while Kell hurried to the bed chamber and returned with blankets and pillows. Skjebne made Sebalrai more comfortable and Kell stretched Fenrir out on a linen sheet. The wulf was not stirring and seemed very close to death.

'Now.' Skjebne softly brushed Sebalrai's hair aside and laid his hand on her brow. She was cold with shock.

There are no wounds on her, Kell. The Sustren did not find her. The blood is Fenrir's . . .

'People came. I heard talking . . .'

'Women's voices?'

Sebalrai nodded and looked at her friends' faces with wide moist eyes.

'Women's voices, but once I heard a man – not Wrynn, a stranger. His voice was harsh and rasping. Feoh was trying to explain something – she talked about Slean I think. The other women – there were two of them at least – sounded as though they didn't believe her. Their tempers were rising. They were shouting. Then one of the chairs was knocked over. I heard scuffling . . . I wanted to come out and help, but I knew it was dangerous . . .'

'You did exactly the right thing, *bearn*. And then?'

'Then the man called out. I think Fenrir had appeared. One of the women screamed. More furniture scraped about. There were noises . . . Fenrir growling. Shouting again. Things bumped on the floor. I heard the door slam shut. Then it was quiet for a long time . . .'

She looked across at the wulf and reached to touch his body. Her lip trembled and tears welled up.

'Will he die, Skjebne? Will he?'

'Don't trouble over that now. Wulves cling to life tightly, as they do their prey.'

'I waited awhile,' she went on. 'And when there were no more sounds I pushed the hatch away and there was that mat covering it. Fenrir was lying over by the wall, just like he is now, hardly breathing.'

'They must have left him for dead,' Kell said, feeling his heart tighten with anger and grief.

'I brought him back to this hideaway with me and pulled the *healm* back over as best I could, and then the hatch. And I held him. I thought that as long as I held him he would hold on to life . . . But . . .'

'So he will, Sebalrai.' Kell stood up and drew out his knife. 'We are already brothers in blood, Fenrir and I,' he said. 'But that was before Wrynn granted us the Draca's power and gave us the Radiant Iron. Without the mage here, or Feoh to work her healing, this is the best I can do.'

So saying, Kell knelt again beside Fenrir and felt in his fur where it was matted with blood. He found the wound he was looking for, one going deep through the muscle to the bone of the wulf's shoulder. There a vessel was still pulsing weakly.

Without hesitation Kell drew the sharp blade across his palm and pressed it firmly to Fenrir's flesh.

For several minutes there was no visible change. But then the wulf jolted and a wave of vitality seemed to spread out from the wound. Amazingly the slashed vein closed up and the bleeding stopped. Kell moved back but still knelt beside his bloodkin, touching Fenrir's head from time to time until the wulf stretched out all his limbs and gave a long heaving sigh and opened his eyes.

The Godwulf sends his blessings to you Kell, and assures us both it is not time yet for me to join him . . .

And Kell struggled to make some kind of witty reply, but could only smile and hug his *wulfenbrooor* close and felt quite ridiculous that no words would come, only tears.

Although Fenrir was healing with astonishing rapidity, he was still too weak to walk unaided. Hora made up a harness of bed blankets and took the wulf's weight on his back for the return journey to the hills. And weakened though she also was, Sebalrai did her best to maintain a shield of veiling, although it was inevitable that the company faded in and out of people's sight as they walked through Kairos – one consolation being that no Slean or Sustren were abroad to pursue them.

'I cannot help but think this is a bad sign,' Hora said. He

went stooped with Fenrir strapped across his shoulders like a beggar carrying all his world's possessions. He looked sideways, left and right. 'The city feels strange to me, quieter than it has been . . .'

'Aye,' Skjebne nodded, as though his own unease had been confirmed. 'And the mists have a peculiar quality, almost like a foggy day. They are sensitive to the mood of the people. I think at some level they know that the evil has come.'

'The Sustren still do not believe they are evil,' Kell said, conveying Fenrir's impressions as they became clear to him. 'The two who came to Feoh's home were surprised, and then angry, that Feoh spoke out against the misuse of the Thrall. But it was the man – one of the Sisters called him Forraedan – who posed the greatest threat. Fenrir thinks he is not a being of flesh and blood –'

'Slean then,' said Skjebne.

'Most likely. He was the one who ordered his minions to take Feoh away. And he it was who struck at Fenrir with a blade when he tried to protect Feoh . . . and there was some kind of stinging dust that Forraedan blew in Fenrir's eyes.'

'But where was Wrynn? Why didn't he try to –'

'Skjebne, Fenrir is telling me that Wrynn did not stay there through the night. He left after we did, to make his arrangements with Dweorg. And he never returned.'

'Because he too fell into the Sustren's trap?' wondered Skjebne, heavy-hearted at the thought. 'Or because he already knew what Forraedan and Orael intended?'

'Wrynn loves Feoh.' That from Sebalrai. 'How can you doubt it? How can you say he deliberately put her at such risk?'

Skjebne felt duly reprimanded – and by a tousle-haired child moreover! – but the suspicion clung to him anyway like a burr that catches on clothing. Yet there was nothing to be gained by arguing one way or another, and so the group fell silent as they left the city behind them and retraced their path to the dell where they had first entered Kairos.

It still seemed miraculous to all of them, even Skjebne who was now quite at home with the wonders of the *ferhocraeft* they had encountered, that a few simple steps could return them to *Windhover*. They walked down into the dell and the view of the city fell away behind them. Here the mists felt tranquil, softened by a pearly light, which grew stronger between the rock spires that was their gateway back to the Orb.

'It occurs to me that many such portals must exist across the world – and beyond it, to the other great orbs wherever they may be.' Skjebne glanced mischievously at Hora. 'When this business is done, my friend, you can go with Thorbyorg and the other wyrda men to meet the rest of the Craeftum and the refugees of Uthgaroar. And you can do it as easily as guzzling a juggon of ale.'

'Well,' Hora grunted, 'if there is ale out there to be guzzled, then maybe I *will* go!'

Kell spoke up. 'It puzzles me why the orbs were needed at all. Couldn't people travel the Sigel Rad simply by using the portals?'

'I have considered this point,' Skjebne said with relish. 'I think that to establish a portal you first need to travel to that point by conventional means. And so the voyagers who walked the Sun's Way at the start of the Wintering of necessity made use of the orbs. Similarly, the wyrda came here originally to create this gateway.'

'There was commerce, then, between the wyrda clan and the people of Kairos?'

'Well, quite possibly Kell. Who knows how readily humankind wandered the world in those days? Maybe, when we have time and opportunity, we can find out.'

Now they had come to the place where the mists were thicker, and where they felt a certain *temptation* to enter them and be engulfed, and so complete their journey.

'We will go to *Windhover* and refresh ourselves there and set our plans – But briefly, for the danger to Feoh is great, and I would not see her suffer any longer than she must.'

'Aye,' Kell added, 'and I desire to meet with the mage Forraedan and pass on Fenrir's reply to his blade.'

So they stepped forward and seemed only to walk a few paces before they had made their unimaginable way back to the orb. And behind them the dell was left empty, but for the mist and the old twisted apple tree and the agate-bees' song.

Thorbyorg and the wyrda men made a great fuss of welcome when Hora and his companions arrived, as did Magula and the wulfen pack over Fenrir, though in their own less vocal way. Then having cleansed themselves and fed with modest fare, Skjebne called a meeting of his friends in *Windhover*'s crystal room, where the light that shone between nowheres suffused the air and seemed to be aware of their discussions . . .

'We have no idea what we may find at the sanctum of the Thrall Makers – and this has been the will of Wierd throughout all of our adventures. We know that the Sustren were there, and still might be; and we know that they have persuaded at least some of the lyblaeca to realise the All Mother's dream.'

'Why don't we assemble our forces and strike as a hammer might crack open a shell!' Thorbyorg wanted to know. Kell found himself smiling at this bluster.

'Because Feoh has most probably been taken there and the Sustren's first act of retaliation would be to kill her. That too might be Wrynn's fate. Besides, First Eolder, our road leads us on to Arcanum, wherever that might be. Remember that Feoh's main purpose in Kairos was to ally herself with the Sustren and glean what she could from them. If she dies, we are left in ignorance.'

'She may not know the location of the Goddess's stronghold.'

'She may not. But the lyblaeca will know – Forraedan and those who have sided with him. So, my suggestion is that we keep our main strength in check until Arcanum. We should send but a few back to Kairos to seek out Feoh and Wrynn – Hora takes his power in combat; Kell takes his wits and Wierd's favour, and his most useful friend Tsep. He also takes the keen edge of Fenrir's revenge – the young wulf himself is still too weak to go, so I wonder if you, Magula, would represent your kin with your gift of keen senses and a crushing jaw?'

'He regards your request as an honour,' Kell said, 'and wonders if you will allow Wulfmaer to accompany us? An *utewulfen* would add another element of safety.'

'That is decided then. My intention is to direct the endeavour with the use of the Guardian Helmet. It occurs to me that so small a party can journey in a single travel orb – and I suspect that we can send it through the portal to the dell above Kairos, and then on to the Thrall Brothers' sanctum. I will muster a force of eye orbs to go with you. They are likely to prove very useful once you reach your destination.'

So with those decisions settled, the final preparations were made. While Hora and Thorbyorg discussed weaponry, Kell retained the knife and accepted the fire weapon that Skjebne presented to him. Then he went to the small peaceful chamber where Fenrir was recovering, and noticed at once the gleam of regret in the wulf's amber eyes.

I would like to come with you. I long to feel Forraedan's neck between my jaws!

I will take your pain with me and hand it back to him, Kell answered. He checked Fenrir's wounds. *The Radiant Iron works its magic well. Soon you will be completely healed.*

That comforts me, of course. But if the blood of the Draca knows itself, and if Wrynn has deceived us as Skjebne half believes, then he will realise you are coming and the extent of the forces you bring.

That possibility will not stop us, Fenrir. We have to go.

I know, Fenrir replied as he looked into Kell's eyes and through them to the temper of the soul that lay beyond. *The Godwulf will talk with you.*

I am strengthened by that honour. And I will stand here before you again very soon.

And it was of immense comfort to Kell that even when he had turned away and Fenrir had passed from his sight, he still felt the wulf's presence riding beside him – or perhaps it was indeed the spirit of the Godwulf as his dear friend had said.

Kell went quickly to the chamber of the travel orbs, and there found the company assembled, together with Sebalrai.

'Skjebne has not changed his mind,' she told him with the brief smile that was a trait of hers, and which it delighted Kell to see. 'I am not going with you to Kairos.'

'I'll feel happier knowing you are safe here . . .'

'And I'll feel happier knowing you are safe home.'

'Then I will hurry back,' he said, and to his consternation found himself blushing – a condition that was hardly helped by the fact that Hora stood close by, grinning at them like a horse.

'I'll be here.' Sebalrai's voice was a whisper and Kell had to lean closer to hear . . . Closer, so that now he smelt the perfume of her hair and felt her breath on his face. Closer, so that she was able to kiss him lightly on the lips and entrance him completely with the way the light caught in her eyes.

Then she moved away back and was but a girlchild again and as coy and flustered as the boy.

'Ho ho!' Hora made a great bellow that startled everyone present. 'With such a token Kell will be invincible in battle!'

'Then let me kiss you also, ironheart,' Sebalrai said in a singsong way – such a wonderful ploy that the colour rose at once to the warrior's cheeks and sent him bustling into the travel orb.

Skjebne came up smiling and put his hand on Kell's shoulder.

'I will be with you through every danger. A dozen eye orbs will accompany you. And they are not passive observers of events. Through the Guardian Helmet's wisdom I have fathomed the nature of the weapons they contain. Also remember you are not there to fight with the Sustren or the lyblaeca, but simply to find Feoh and Wrynn and return them to us. Now go with all speed.'

Kell boarded the travel orb, the hatch closed briskly and the stout heart of the machine began to beat in a steady rhythm. He sat with Hora before the control table that was tilted to their view. It was busy with lights, but their mysterious nature was of no consequence, since Skjebne was controlling the vehicle remotely.

The machine shifted slightly; there was a bump and a slow easy swaying, though no sensation of speed. Behind Kell Wulfmaer gave a small whimpering sigh since this room and its angles and shadows and smells were all strange to him. Magula soothed him with a balm of thought.

The orb's gentle movement and the subdued humming in the room continued for a time and began to lull Kell towards slumber – until the forward viewscreen unshielded itself like an opening eye to show them the outside world.

'By the Rad,' breathed Hora in amazement. They had already come through the portal, and the dell where Feoh had met them earlier was swiftly dropping from view. Almost at once the prospect was snatched away as the orb swung in a different direction and the mists of Kairos swirled like a cloak all around. Kell noticed a number of the smaller eye orbs hurtling close beside them before the mist whisked them from view.

'The Thrall Makers' settlement in the hills isn't far from here,' Kell said for the wulves' benefit. And the words were barely spoken when the travellers felt a sensation of falling and the orb dropped clear of the fogs . . .

And the pale elegant spires and buildings they had seen from a distance in Kairos now appeared directly below them, perhaps five hundred spans away.

Kell scanned the scene to make swift sense of it. An empty road swept away from the settlement towards the city. All was defended by a high boundary wall. Nothing seemed to be moving in or around the sanctum. There were clusters of smaller dwellings and larger meeting places. Their style and generous use of glass reminded Kell of the Tutorium at Perth . . . There were groves and parks; a small lake near one of the well-tended gardens . . . There were secluded quadrangles that seemed private and serene . . . And courtyards for gatherings, and . . .

Kell's attention was drawn to a group of dark roundish objects in one of the courtyards; and for a moment he thought it was some kind of odd decoration before he realised that he was looking down on three of the lens-shaped sky craft of the Slean.

10

Uvavnuk's Song

'They may not have seen us.' That was Skjebne's voice, speaking to them as though out of the very air.

Why so few? Kell wondered. Three ships were not an impossible obstacle.

Immediately the travel orb streaked in a vast loop away from the sanctum and lost height quickly as it did so. Skjebne also deployed the eye orbs in a wide scatter throughout the settlement, keeping them close to shadows and walls.

'I will have the travel orb primed ready for your return; and I'll have an eye orb accompany you, so that we may stay in contact and you can see what the other orbs see.'

'Hopefully we can find Feoh very shortly . . .'

With two wulfen tracking her, that will be very shortly indeed, Magula said with just the merest hint of pique.

Skjebne brought the travel orb down towards a small woodland bordering one of the parks on the settlement's fringe. Carefully it sank among the trees and came to rest on a bed of bracken, supported just above the ground by its motivating field. As the hatch folded out, the company caught sight of a single eye orb bobbing patiently in the air nearby, and at a distance beyond it the outermost buildings of the sanctum glinted in the pale hazy sunlight of Kairos.

Magula stood at the threshold and read the story of the breeze, and then Wulfmaer slid past him and almost instantly vanished into the ferns. His job would be to explore and to stalk alone, relaying his impressions constantly to the pack leader.

Wulfmaer says there is no immediate danger. We can approach the place of the slow-eyes now . . .

They left the orb and made their way through the wood as far as it curved towards the sanctum. Magula moved silently beside them; and Kell could feel the wulf's restrained exasperation at Hora's clumping tread. The warrior paused once to readjust the multiblade which was his primary weapon, and to don a leather headshield that protected his skull and the back of his neck. The multiblade buzzed quietly, holding its energies ready. Hora changed his grip on the handle and the metals reconfigured and the thing became a sword, curved like the She-Wulf-Claw-Moon, deadly and sleek.

Why does Hora go as though to battle? Magula wondered to Kell. He did not possess Fenrir's greater tolerance of the slow-eyes' limitations. *Wulfmaer has already confirmed this area is safe.*

Because we do not have your abilities or speed, it is a sensible precaution for us to be constantly in readiness. Hora isn't wise to your ways yet, Magula. Be as patient with him as you are easy in your power . . .

Well . . . tell him to stay primed. Wulfmaer has reached the outer precincts and there found something interesting.

Kell relayed this to Skjebne who sent two eye orbs converging on the scene. Through the screens of the orb that accompanied them, Kell and the others were able to look upon what the *utewulfen* had found – a spring that trickled out of a vertical face of moss-covered rock and ran in a glittering thread among stones. It gathered briefly in a shallow pool before vanishing again into the ground.

And beside the pond a woman knelt and sang –

'The great sea has sent me on my way, cast me adrift, moves me like a whirl of water through Wierd's ocean . . . Under the high-built hall and through the mightiness of storms the spirit moves within me . . . Now I am carried far away, trembling with terror, trembling with joy, as the great sea sends me on my journey . . .'

The rhythms of the song were complex and subtle, almost random like the music of the stream. But the melodies sounded as simple as a child's innocence and as clear as the water in the pool. And the woman sang entranced by the weave of the words, oblivious of the wulf that crouched listening, its head cocked curiously to one side, but ready nonetheless to leap and tear out her throat.

Presently a small group approached the sacred site and respected its sanctity and stayed some steps back from the water. There was a huge man, square shouldered, armoured for war: his beard was startlingly red and his face and hands were decorated with blue tattoos. In front of him and side by side there stood a tall fair youth, fresh in his musk of manhood: and a strong, lean *eoldenwulf*, a little grey around the muzzle and well rooted in his history of blood, but yet with enormous wisdom in his eyes . . . And there was something else about the boy; some other creature lay hidden about him, a mischievous thing, very intelligent and unexpectedly dangerous . . . And in the air nearby floated a spherical contrivance of dark metal and shining glass, which even as the singer became aware of it unsheathed a growth of blades that made it a fearsome weapon indeed.

Despite this arrival, the woman sang on until the ritual was completed. Her voice faded slowly until it blended with the trickling of the stream. She looked upon the strangers without fear, because her greater sadness overwhelmed all other emotions on this day.

'What are you doing, *sweostor*? Can we ask that without offending you?' Kell kept his voice low, because there was a gentleness to this place: it was hallowed ground and had been so for a very long time.

'Well, I am praying. And you do not offend me, youth, because you have shown regard for where I am and what I do.'

She was a pretty woman, Kell thought; tall and rather thin (as far as he could make out, because her green robes were voluminous), her hair long and dark, and her complexion very pale. There was something immensely tragic about her. It touched the boy's heart directly and made a mark there that would take a long time fading.

'You are frightened of me,' she added unexpectedly. 'All of you, in your own ways, are afraid.'

'There is no creature that looks upon tomorrow who is not afraid,' Kell replied, speaking Magula's words. 'We know you are Sustren. What frightens you?'

She smiled, and it was a ghastly smile, full of pain.

'Perhaps knowing what I have become. Perhaps not knowing what will become of me.'

'Do you know why we are here?' asked Hora. He looked a little self-conscious in his war-gear, the great cutting edge of the multiblade shining in the morning's fuzzy light.

'You are here to find your sister, who is also a sister of mine.'

'Yes.' Kell came closer. 'Tell us where she is.'

'Lost!' It was almost a wail. 'I think we are all lost now!'

I have an image of Feoh from this woman's mind, Kell, Magula said, though for some reason he kept it hidden inside himself. *And even below that, deeper in her brain, there is confusion over the Goddess and her work with the Thrall Brothers . . . Slean. I keep seeing Slean, like an echo . . .*

'Will you tell me your name?' Kell spoke gently, as you might to a wounded child. The woman clenched a fist and the sharp fingernails dug deep, and she let her blood drip slowly into the shimmering pool.

'And what would you do with it if I gave it to you? How will it help you in your search?'

'Perhaps it won't. I am called Kell.'

'And now what shall I do with that name? Maybe I'll toss it like a coin on to the hoard that is my memory, and there let it lie.'

'Spend it when you feel the need,' Kell said briefly, for now the woman infuriated him and he felt she was lost only in her own self-sorrow.

He started to turn aside, and in that moment Magula swept through her mind, revealing this power to her, and came away knowing where Feoh was held, and knowing Wrynn's fate and that of the woman whose last minutes would pass by in solitude.

Feoh needs us now, the wulf's mindvoice snapped like a whip. *She is being kept in the inner precincts.*

He sent a silent direction to Wulfmaer and took lead of the group, drawing them away from the quiet place where the singer hardly noticed their going. Presently, confused and fearful, she lowered her face into the pool to be close to her All Mother, and soon moved on like a whirl of water through Wierd's endless ocean.

Although she was Sustren, her heart was tight with disapproval. Yes, the Sisterhood has seduced and corrupted the lyblaeca, but some of the mages, in turn, have been using this liaison for mercenary ends.

You mean that not all of the Sustren wish to see the Goddess brought into the flesh?

Kell, it is the manner *of her reincarnation they find so unspeakable . . .*

And Magula told what he had learned, and Kell's hatred of the All Mother knew no bounds.

The company moved unchallenged into the spacious halls and passageways of the sanctum. Only once did Kell catch sight of Wulfmaer as he glided like a ghost in the shadow of a wall far in the distance; but his voice was constant in Magula's head, and those pieces of intelligence the eolderwulf thought were of use he passed on to Hora and Kell.

Nevertheless, despite Wulfmaer's astonishing tracking ability, it was Skjebne's sweep-searching with the eye orbs that came across Feoh first. Without pause for explanation he guided the orb that accompanied them in the direction of his discovery: Magula paced easily, but Kell and especially Hora needed all their stamina and strength to keep up.

They ran along empty echoing corridors, bypassing many rooms. The doors to some of these were left open, and the scattered books and papers and the toppled furniture within told of great haste and confusion.

'Where are the Thrall Makers?' he wondered aloud, for they saw not a soul on the way. 'And the other Sustren?'

'Kell –' That was Skjebne. 'Using the eye orbs I have come across two lyblaeca slain. Another lies dying out in the grounds. There has been terrible violence here. I have no explanation for this, except perhaps that they resisted the All Mother's will, and that of Forraedan the betrayer.'

'What about Feoh?'

'She is near. Take care, for there are Slean . . . and Forraedan himself – Forraedan.'

More slowly now, more cautiously, the group moved on and came to a large open vestibule where flights of stone steps curved up to higher galleries and rooms. Kell spotted Wulfmaer standing at the top of one such stairway, and nearby two eye orbs with their defensive blades deployed hung steady in the air. Kell smiled to think of Skjebne's pleasure in discovering that little trick.

Magula left his friends and streaked up the stairs, as lightly and as silently as the wind. Together he and Wulfmaer found the room they were seeking within seconds.

Two Slean, and Forraedan . . .

There was more, and Kell caught a glimpse of it through the pack leader's eyes before Magula veiled the horror. But it was a misplaced consideration on the wulf's part; for Kell was hardly a child any more and knew he must look upon the faces of evil to assess his own strengths and goodness.

'Assemble some more of the eye orbs, Skjebne,' he advised quietly. 'And have them come armed.'

Then he drew his fire weapon from its belt and followed the wulfen call, with Hora just a pace behind.

As they moved along the gallery they heard voices – the

harsh tones of the mage, and Feoh's softer and more muffled voice, heavy with exhaustion and pain.

'By the very heart of Wierd she will pay for this . . .' Kell whispered as the revulsion rose in him again; for in his mind's eye it was clear now exactly what the All Mother had done, and a moment later they came to the room of Feoh's torment and saw her for themselves.

She was shackled to a star-shaped frame propped vertically, and her clothes had been largely torn from her body and her flesh had been beaten and cut. Even now Forraedan touched a silver wand to her leg, and ligetu fuzzed and sparked and the woman shrieked to heaven.

But most shockingly, the lyblaeca and his Slean attendants had removed Feoh's ceramic mask and revealed the ruin of her face: self-inflicted, she had suffered the injury in tearing free the network of threads that had linked her to the Goddess. But now the filaments had been replaced and reached upwards, quivering and shining, to the domed roof of the chamber, which was carved of pure weorthan and reflected Feoh's every tortured thought.

It was one of the Slean guards who first noticed the intruders standing at the threshold. He was completely armoured, the smooth polished helmet revealing nothing of the eyes or face. But clearly he could see, for with a warning bark he alerted his fellow and the mage.

But even as Forraedan turned in startlement and the Slean levelled their weapons, Skjebne sent the eye orb hurtling forward. The appearance of blades was only part of its capability: as it rushed on it loosed a spray of cutting edges that shot with great precision towards the sentinel's body. Three of the knives glanced off the armour and went spinning and tinkling across the floor. A fourth sliced clean through the steel and lodged in the arm; another buried itself completely in the Slean's chest and disappeared from view.

And the man staggered and bent forward as though defeated, but then recovered, stood upright with his fire-rod coming to bear.

Kell acted quickly, firing twice, both to the head. The helmet exploded and the body toppled backwards and fell with a crash.

Hora dealt with the second guard. A panicky shot from the Slean caught the warrior's hand and took two fingers away. But the spill of blood and the scalding pain simply gave the man greater resolve. Despite Magula's earlier impression of Hora's cloddish tread, his wyrda training spared him now – Hora seemed almost to squat on his haunches, dipping down and then up with a powerful spring, turning, whirling, his right arm extended with the multiblade shining like a half-circle of glittering light. It hardly made a sound as it cut through metal and what passed for flesh; and even before Hora had completed his move fully a third of the Slean's body dropped away, the dismembered arm twitching briefly before it was still.

Another scything blow, equally fast, Hora sweeping the blade low, completed the attack and the guard's body was scattered to the room's four corners.

And then the frenzy of rage seemed to ebb and Hora looked around and saw Kell standing motionless perhaps ten paces from Forraedan. Closer to, the wolves held their position, hunkered down and ready to leap.

'I can kill her with a touch,' the mage announced. He held the ligetu wand a fingerwidth from Feoh's head. And his arm was so steady and so still that the wand did not quiver at all.

Kell took this time to assess him. Forraedan was equally as tall as Wrynn, though some past injury or perhaps the circumstances of his birth had twisted his spine and left him crooked. His hair was pure white, grown long in the style of the lyblaeca and twined up in a rope crisscrossed with leather thong. His skin was pale and seemed lifeless, and was decorated with a number of sigils that looked luminous beneath the weorthan light. Like Wrynn, Forraedan favoured the flowing robes of the Thrall Maker guild, in this case coloured a sumptuous crimson.

'Lay down the weapons, and have the eye orb withdraw!' his voice cracked out, shattering the spell. He gazed with contempt at the wulves. 'And bring these animals to heel. Do it now, *lytling*, to save your *sweostor* some pain.'

They did as they were commanded. Magula and Wulfmaer stood and loped back until they stood behind Kell, who laid his fire weapon down. Hora did the same with the multiblade, and Skjebne retracted the eye orb's barbs.

'So, the wyrm Wrynn told you much, and you have found me out more quickly than I expected. But you are too late in all ways, Kell the little ploughboy whose only power lies in his luck. The hyrnetu will have reacted to the death of their Slean masters and even now are on their way: soon you will be dead and then I claim my reward for aiding the Goddess in her work, and for removing this thorn in her side.'

'Was there any need to do this to Feoh?' Kell's voice was very calm, a thin veil concealing his fear, but more importantly his fury.

'The lady has been stubborn. Besides, the All Mother wanted to know the contents of her mind. And she will, through the contrivance of the weorthan glass. She will soon understand the extent of your threat – if there is to be any threat, once the hyrnetu have cut you to shreds.'

'The Thrall Brothers will punish you for this!'

Forraedan's laughter echoed back down from the vaulted roof, which glowed and swirled and began to form patterns, almost like something alive.

'The Thrall Brothers have been destroyed, but for those lyblaeca who will aid me in completing the All Mother's final work. They have already been taken to Arcanum. And when the Goddess walks in the world again, I will return here and claim Kairos as my own.'

As the mage was speaking, a very curious thing had been going on. Kell felt a stirring in his chest, and had noticed the way the weorthan seemed to be building towards some expression of Feoh's mind. He realised now that even while the glass had been drawing out her thoughts, she in turn was manipulating the matrix to her own will.

And at that moment her understanding was clarified. She had read Tsep's intention and held back her knowledge – but used it now as a distraction to make the deed possible. The crystal dome bloomed with the sight of what was about to happen: Forraedan could not help but glance up, and that was when the man-bat acted; squirming free of Kell's tunic, launching himself in the air and across those few spans of intolerable daylight to the lyblaeca's face. Too late Forraedan tried to bring the ligetu wand to bear – Tsep was already inside its arc and avoided it easily, driven as he was by his instincts both to save his friend's kin and to return to the darkness.

He entered through the mage's startled eye.

Forraedan's scream pierced to the furthest corners of the sanctum: and it was the most chilling noise that Kell had ever heard, because it was filled with awareness of the terrible thing that was happening, as much as the agony it brought.

But Tsep's mission was not to torment. His work was quick. He disappeared from view, and a moment later the life left the Thrall Maker's body – or whatever had passed for life within the alien substance that was the flesh of the Slean. The vicious silver wand slipped to the stone floor and sputtered and snapped as its energies discharged. Forraedan's body crumpled and he leaned over on to his side, curling in death like a withering leaf or a child in an attitude of sleep.

A stream of curses immediately issued from the eye orb as Skjebne vented his rage and frustration. Hora acted more practically. He snatched up his multiblade and severed the gleaming threads linking Feoh to the weorthan. The crystal dome blazed up briefly before all its light faded away. Together he and Kell loosened the woman's restraining straps and lowered her gently down. Then Kell retrieved little Tsep, scooping him up and tucking him back inside the tunic pouch.

'Wrynn.' Feoh gasped out the name. The end of the ordeal had brought an overwhelming exhaustion. She was barely conscious. 'I cannot see Wrynn . . .'

'We have no time to waste.' Hora went over to Forraedan, dragged off his crimson robe, wrapped it around Feoh and lifted her up in his arms.

Wulfmaer and Magula meanwhile had vanished from sight – only to reappear just then with alarm thoughts flashing through Kell's head . . .

But he needed no telling, for they could all hear the busy noise of the hyrnetu as they drew nearer; the screeching of many metal limbs upon the marble floors.

Back aboard *Windhover*, immersed in the world of the Guardian Helmet, Skjebne looked upon the halls and corridors of the sanctum through a hundred anxious eyes. Forraedan's rearguard force had consisted of perhaps ten Slean warriors – two of them now slain – three ships, and a swarm of hyrnetu. Perhaps a score of the creatures were now gathering in the vestibule of the building where Kell and the others would soon be impossibly trapped.

'You have to go to the higher levels! I will send the travel orb to get you!'

Skjebne's voice cracked through the almost ecstatic paralysis that had gripped Kell at the sound of the hyrnetu's proximity.

'But Wrynn –'

'I have not found him,' Skjebne reported.

He is here in this building, Magula said. *We smell his traces.*

'Then Hora, do as Skjebne has bidden. Go as high as you can –'

'There are balconies attached to the uppermost rooms. I will have the eye orbs accompany you for protection.'

'And one for us,' Kell said with a flashing smile that had no joy in it at all. 'Let us go now, and may Wierd guide our way.'

So they parted, with no certainty of seeing each other again. Kell spared a few moments to watch Hora loping with little effort, though dripping blood from his wounded hand, up the curving stairs to the higher rooms. The single small orb floating with him was joined by another a few moments later; then a third, and a fourth.

'And one for you.'

Kell looked round at the sphere that hung in the air an armspan away. 'Thank you Skjebne.'

Now quickly, Magula said. *This way.*

Fortunately their route took them away from the vestibule where the hyrnetu were clustering. Wulfmaer ran on ahead with a soft pattering of claws: Magula forced himself to slow down to match Kell's fastest pace.

How far?

He is not far away, the wulf replied. *Wulfmaer is already with him. But Kell – you should know . . .*

There was no need for the words to be formed; the feeling that accompanied them, the sense of regret and sadness, said enough.

They came to a side corridor and followed it along to an annexe that led in its turn to a magnificent hall decorated with fine stone columns and huge dark tapestries woven with esoteric designs. Like the room where Forraedan had been, this too featured a dome of elegantly spun glass; though in this case not weorthan. The fathomless mists of Kairos swirled beyond it, filled with light but concealing the sun beyond.

Perhaps this was a place where the lyblaeca had conducted their mysterious rituals, repatterning life to create new forms. And perhaps it had been difficult work, far more intricate than the labour of killing . . .

Wrynn lay supine on a granite block. His face looked peaceful and his arms were resting at his sides. His chest had been opened with some efficient cutting tool, and his ribs split apart, and his heart removed. It lay on a silver dish placed above his solar plexus.

Kell gave a soft groan, not so much at the loss of a friend but in anticipation of Feoh's further pain at this news. Losing Kano had damaged her deeply: to have Wrynn taken too might finally destroy her.

The wulves waited until the first wave of grief had passed from the boy. They understood human ways enough to show this respect. Then, as Wulfmaer returned to the entranceway, Magula padded over to the mage and bent his head low and sniffed at his mouth and eyes, and then at the grey heart that lay so utterly still.

He is not dead, the wulf pronounced, so calmly and with such full assurance that Kell wanted to laugh.

Don't you feel it yourself, Kell? Don't you recognise the subtle touch of the Radiant Iron? I know of it only because you conferred that gift upon Fenrir – and all wulves in the pack work as one mind.

I – I don't know what I feel. Kell took a step closer to Wrynn, to that awful sight.

He will be a long time in the healing. But unlike the slow-eyes of ordinary flesh and blood, Wrynn's life does not reside entirely within the cells.

I do not understand you.

I do not fully understand myself.

Magula lifted his head and looked up and his eyes shone like two moons.

The power is stirring in him now . . . No, not in him . . . It approaches!

Hwaet! The hyrnetu!

Wulfmaer came hurrying back in the slipstream of his thoughts.

'Skjebne – what can you do for us?'

The eye orb that had come with them dipped in agitation.

'Kell. I can send a second travel orb to meet you. There is no safe way out of the sanctum that I can see. Go on to the roof and wait. If the hyrnetu get that far you will have to keep them back.'

'But I don't think we –'

'There is something else.' Skjebne sounded strange; elated it seemed –

And Wulfmaer yelped a warning as the first of the hyrnetu scuttled into the room.

Immediately Kell drew out his fire weapon and discharged a pulse of light that sprayed amongst the creature's angled limbs. It was hurled over backwards and lay twitching like a grotesque grey hand.

A second insect, upright like a mantis, sprang into sight and leaped forward. Kell's next shot took it glancingly. It tumbled away and crashed down, but crawled on towards its target, its eyes globed and glassy black. Instantly Wulfmaer was upon it, wrenching at its limbs. Magula hurled himself at a third hyrnetu. But another and yet another clamoured to be into the room.

And then all meaning fled away from this petty battle as the whole hall darkened. Kell risked an instant to take stock, and howled at the sight of some monstrous thing dropping swiftly from the sky towards them.

Wulfmaer was already moving. Magula assessed Kell's need of help, then dived with him to take shelter beside the granite altar as the Draca crashed through the crystal dome in a downpour of glass and settled lightly in the midst of the scrambling hyrnetu.

It was huge, powerful, awesome in its towering strength; silver-grey like fire-brushed chrome, but flecked and streaked with glints of colour as it stood and filled the room and looked impassively upon these worthless scurrying things.

Nevertheless, through stupidity or the compulsion of their controlling force, the hyrnetu launched an attack. At least a dozen sprouted wings that appeared with a crackling of metals and came spinning up towards the dragon's head.

It moved with the ease and fluidity of quicksilver, taking several of the insects into its mouth and crunching them to pieces in its jaws. Others it flicked away with its pinioned claws, sending them smashing into fragments against the walls. The Draca turned, swept its wings around and hurled most of the remaining hyrnetu to destruction . . .

A few escaped the damage and scampered beneath the dragon's vast form and rushed towards Kell and the wolves.

Kell dispatched one of them with his fire weapon, reducing it to a quivering pile of sticklike legs and smoking shell. Magula and Wulfmaer each battled with another of the hyrnetu, achieving victories but at the cost in Wulfmaer's case of a deep slash above his left eye.

Now! Now is our chance!

Magula had spotted a spiral of stone steps half hidden by drapes behind the altar, and could smell the sweet cool spill of fresh air rushing down them. His thought lashed across Kell's mind, causing Kell instantly to retreat and make for the steps – but then he stopped and took time to watch the Draca, the being of Radiant Iron, loom above Wrynn and lower itself, and somehow enfold the mage within its substance. When it stood proud again, Wrynn the Thrall Maker was gone.

The Draca lifted its head and arched its neck back and emitted a call of exquisite terror and beauty that rang and vibrated through the walls and ceilings to the very foundations of the sanctum. Its colossal wings began to unfurl –

And Kell was running with his wulfen *brooor* madly up the spiralled way, round and round, twisting and twisting upwards to a door that stood open on to a broad balcony; a peaceful place shaded and secluded by vellum plants and spreading vines.

But behind them came the insane rattling of hyrnetu limbs on stone, while above the shadow of the Draca flashed by and went vertically upwards into the haze, dragging rags and tatters of mist in its wake.

Kell swept his gaze across the panorama of the sanctum and the grounds far below, but it was through Wulfmaer's razor-keen eyes that he spotted the dark disc of the travel orb hurrying towards them – and coming in at an angle to intercept it, two of the three Slean ships they had earlier seen.

Be ready to board!

He turned to face the stairway and moved to its lip, firing streaks of light down into the darkness. A glow of flame and red-hot stone and the stink of scorched metal rose up in reply – but also the shrieks and chitterings of yet more hyrnetu that had appeared after the dragon's departure.

Kell discharged the weapon again and again, until it grew hot in his hand and its energies started to falter.

Kell! It is time!

The boy spun round and saw the orb closing in a wide swoop . . . And the nearer of the two Slean craft close behind it . . . *And a second orb dropping like a stone to intercept it!*

Kell whooped at Skjebne's clever ploy. A second later the orb crashed headlong into the Slean craft and the two fell away, spinning and burning through veils of dark smoke to the quiet precincts below.

'Quickly, go aboard.' Skjebne's voice, issuing simultaneously from an eye orb that had just joined them, and the other travel orb that now held itself hovering just a span from the balcony edge.

Wulfmaer went first, leaping lightly up on to the stone balustrade and then across the divide and into the orb. Magula followed a heartbeat later.

Kell scrambled up on to the parapet as a clutch of hyrnetu reached the top of the stairway and burst out on to the balcony. That distraction and the dizzying drop to the ground caused his concentration to waver. He felt himself misjudge the jump, felt himself freeze at the sight of the distant trees and the ground a hundred spans beneath, and the black mangle and fire of the crashed ships. He was free in the air and all of the past and future and all-that-there-was became concentrated into this instant of incomparable life!

Then the orb's nurturing fields as much as Magula's strong jaws plucked him from the death plunge. Kell saw the balcony and the high-pitched roof of the sanctum tilt and turn as the hatchway closed. There was a brief and sickening swoop to his stomach as the orb accelerated away, sending him tumbling off balance.

He scrambled the short distance to the front of the vessel and struggled into the pilot's chair and watched the ground streak by through the orb's forward viewport. The rocks and hills, the trees and stretches of wildland were smeared by speed.

'Not long, not far,' came Skjebne's reassuring voice.

But immediately afterwards the sky lit up with a great flash and the orb rocked and seemed to kick to one side. The Slean pursuit ship was firing upon it.

Kell turned towards the wulves; and while Magula sat hunkered with his face impassive, Wulfmaer had some uncertainty in his pale-golden eyes.

A second strike hammered into the orb. This time the whole earth was snatched from sight, reappearing a second later much closer. A bolt of light zipped by and dredged up earth and rocks below and a little ahead of the speeding ship.

And then Kell thought he recognised the lie of the ground – and there, yes – the green cleft of the dell with its craggy spires – and the unfolding fog and the reassuring glow of the portal.

Skjebne must have been working on his instincts, Kell thought, and became unaccountably calm as another Slean firebolt engulfed the orb and sent it diving towards the ground into the flickering mists in a glory of thunder and flame.

11

Gebedraedan

Feoh felt herself lifted up and up towards an all-encompassing light. It was featureless, penetrating her every cell, and yet it contained all the meaning of the universe folded into the tiniest part of an instant of time; higher up, further in, until she seemed to look upon the face of Wierd itself and knew her fate and the destiny of her children and on through all the generations of human life to *Ragnarokrr*, the great and final twilight of the stars.

Perhaps it was the cosmic light that blinded her, or perhaps the sight of her friends gathered round as she woke, but Feoh found herself weeping without the will to stop, or the desire to do so; cried until young Sebalrai bent and hugged her tight in the comfort that only women know and understand, while the men stood back subdued until the healing was over.

Now, using an instinctive ability that was as sure and elegant as any wulfen's, Feoh swept her attention through the minds of those gathered there, and learned of Wrynn's fate and the part that the Draca had played. And no words were spoken about it, for none would have been equal to the task.

Skjebne, looking pale and shaken by recent events, came forward and held Feoh's hand, before she could utter any complaint or feel in the least self-conscious, he kissed her face on both sides, and smiled at her, and stood away.

'He will be taken back to Hugauga,' she said, speaking of Wrynn. 'There the Draca will endeavour to revive him — because he is not dead, only lost for a while. Everything he was lives on in the Radiant Iron.'

And Skjebne nodded as though he believed that, but wondered deep inside himself whether even the Radiant Iron could revive flesh so terribly torn. This suspicion must exist in Feoh's heart also, but for the rest she was being brave or maybe choosing not to look along that dark road.

'Well,' Skjebne said, treading lightly with his words, 'our way is towards Arcanum. But when this last battle has been fought and won we will take you to Hugauga and your love . . . But you must help us now, Feoh, to understand the difference between the qualities of the Draca, and the process that makes men into Slean. This, I feel, is most important.'

Feoh nodded and sat up a little in her bed, readjusting her position so that she could see Hora with his hand bandaged up standing near the doorway, and loyal Fenrir and Magula just beyond. They had all survived, then, this far.

'Realise this, that the *ferhocraeft* that creates the Slean has nothing to do with the nature of Radiant Iron, or with normal flesh–and–blood life. During their centuries of relative isolation in Kairos, the Thrall Makers uncovered many unusual ways of mimicking the vitality of things. The result of one such became the Slean. These are beings, once alive, now caught in life's reflection; not living, not dead, and therefore not able to die in the sense that we understand –'

Their spirits, then, do not move on? Magula asked.

'I cannot even say with any truth that they possess their original spirits. A creature that is Slean will have an identity and a sense of self-awareness. And so Forraedan would say that he was Forraedan, and to all intents and purposes would behave that way . . .'

'Did we kill him?' Tsep had prompted the question through Kell.

'Enough damage was done to unstitch whatever force animated him. Once that happens, a Slean cannot be brought back.' Feoh smiled ominously. 'At least, the lyblaeca have not managed it yet.'

'So the All Mother sent the Sustren to Kairos to persuade the Thrall Brothers to reveal the secret of the Slean . . .'

'Yes Skjebne. What use would it be to the Goddess to enter the body of Shamra, only to have that body age and die within an eyeblink of time?'

'This was my greatest fear.' Skjebne sighed heavily and half-glanced at Kell but would not look him fully in the eye. 'That after all these ordeals, we would recover Shamra – only to find she was Shamra no more.'

Their hearts were not helped by dwelling on such matters. There was a great deal of work to be done, and Skjebne stirred himself to instruct the others. He found Thorbyorg and had the First Eolder gather together his wyrda men – twenty of them and a half dozen boars – and in the crystal room explained as much as he knew of the Slean and the hyrnetu, and those among the lyblaeca they would find in Arcanum. Skjebne knew that the warriors relished the prospect of battle, but their enemies now were diverse and by-and-large not mortal men – indeed, not all of them would be men, for the Sustren too would surely fight like Valkyries in those last desperate hours for love of their Goddess.

'I also feel by instinct that the All Mother herself will not be vanquished by simple force and the tactics of war. She has had thousands of seasons to prepare for her emergence into the world. Surely, if we can destroy enough of her minions we might delay her plans for many lifetimes . . . But stopping her entirely will be by other means than a blade. However, I do feel that much of her Slean force was depleted at Hugauga and then at Kairos.'

Skjebne's plan – and Thorbyorg agreed – was to have the wyrda force arrive in the other great orb, in *Skymaster*. From there they could deploy themselves at short notice, in light of the circumstances they found.

'We must also consider that if we and the wulfen aboard *Windhover* are destroyed, there will still be some hope of victory left in the speed and strength of your strike.'

Sitting just a little way off from Skjebne, Magula relayed all of these things to his wulfen pack, and to Fenrir who had remained with Kell and Tsep, Sebalrai and Feoh.

'We too are diverse,' Kell said, prompted by his *wulfenbrooor's* thoughts. 'And our strengths are numerous. The orbs themselves have immense capabilities – Skjebne's eyes will be everywhere when the time comes. And the pack's onemindedness will be vital in our assault upon the Goddess . . .'

'And I will help you as best I can – yes, I am well enough,' Feoh said, noticing Kell's wary expression. 'Better than I was, for I am no longer linked to the All Mother –' (Her hand flickered unknowingly to the ravaged side of her face) '– and I have Wrynn's agony to avenge. Do you suppose that *anybody* could stop me fighting at your side!'

'Nobody would dare,' Sebalrai laughed. 'And I too will be proud to –'

'Well, I don't think that is a good idea.'

Kell suddenly looked very disapproving; and while Feoh was tempted to laugh at the severity of his scowl, instead she gestured to Fenrir and, easing herself from her bed, she and the wulf left the room, with Tsep fluttering bemusedly behind.

Once they had gone, Sebalrai's own temper rose. Her face flushed and there was a spark in her eye that Kell had noticed on other occasions, and knew then that he could not win this clash.

'Sebalrai, for your own sake –'

'If it's *my* own sake then it's mine!' she announced firmly, throwing Kell into puzzlement. 'I am free of Chertan the bandit these many moonths, and nobody owns me now. I will do as I choose and see fit! You kept me from going to the sanctum. You cannot deny me again.'

'I am only thinking to keep you safe.'

'Or because, when we find Shamra, you will have to decide between us?'

'What do you mean? Sebalrai, you know how I feel about you . . .'

'Yes, because we have been through much together and isn't it true that the fear of danger brings people closer – but you and Shamra are heartbonded, you have pledged your life to her.'

'It was a pledge made in another time, in another place, under the shadow of a deceitful Goddess. Shamra and I will decide what our promises mean, as and when I find her and face her as I'm facing you now. In Perth my whole life was a lie. I wouldn't lie to you now, and put you through that pain. I truly love you Sebalrai. I would not want to hurt you in any way.'

His simple honesty made his words the strongest and the best they could be, and Sebalrai had no answer to them but to accept their truth. She looked away from Kell and her eyes grew moist and her face tried to be grown up and proud and understanding and not frightened all at the same time. And Kell took the moment and held her tightly there in that small room, in a wondrous vessel that floated through impossible space somewhere between yesterday and tomorrow.

Skjebne, the all-seer, gazed upon the Guardian Helmet in the room of controls aboard *Windhover*. He was entirely alone by his own choosing, and knew that he was walking the coward's road in not facing his friends in the flesh. For him the time demanded cool thoughts and not the heat of parting. He was alone, and yet his mind through the miracles of the Helmet and the orbs put him in touch with every one of the souls who journeyed with him to this final confrontation.

He turned the helmet this way and that, and though his artisan's eyes appreciated the craft of the wrought metal and the delicate woven filaments within, his soul felt stunned by the accomplishment of the thing – forged so far back in time that the world itself then was an entirely different place; a place he wondered about anew. All of humanity had fought to keep its treasures intact, its heart-hoard safe. That enterprise had been worthy of the winning: the Ice had been outfaced and its merciless fist was at last ungripping the globe. The present horror was human in its making, and its cruelty would be greater and its dominion more dreadful than any winter storm. And if the Goddess were allowed to live beyond this coming conflict, then the world would change again to an even bleaker and more alien land than the glaciers had brought.

Skjebne the all-seer, Skjebne the ordinary man, traced his fingers around the Helmet and came to know its symmetry in his blood. In colour and feel it was something like bronze, but even after centuries the metal remained completely untarnished. The skullcap was plain, but the side plates and brow ridges and nose guard were all decorated with the symbols of the Wyrda Craeftum; *eofor* and blades and orb icons and glyphs that told of the Sun's Way, and the journeys that had been and were yet to be. The destiny of the Helmet was wrought upon its face: that is true of every man.

Skjebne lowered it over his head and knew now where his future lay.

There were no portals to Arcanum. That, perhaps, had been part of its creators' original plan. It lay dreaming in a wilderness of ice beyond the first and original forest, among a nest of mountainous crags – and within them, deep inside to the roots of the rock, and deeper still where rods of eternal steel drew up heat from the shining heart of the planet. It lay twined like a wary serpent around the hoard of its deeds; and somewhere there the eyes of the All Mother watched with a passionless gleam, waiting for the retribution that she knew was bound to come.

At one certain moment that was otherwise no different

from any other, the bleak grey cloudscapes above the city at the end of the world blazed briefly, and then gathered their shadows about themselves again.

Standing in the crystal room in *Windhover*, Kell and his true friends Fenrir and Tsep watched the surging wave of light flash away through the gloom as the energies of their arrival dispersed. Instantly a vast blizzard stormed about the glass in an endlessness of flakes.

Then the viewpoint changed, not in its perspective but in its emphasis. By some clever trick of the crystal, the obscurity thinned to a faint and shimmering distraction, and there far below was Arcanum's mountain fastness bordered on three sides by ice-shattered wasteland, and on the fourth by sheer towering cliffs that dropped straight for a thousand spans into the surging, foaming ocean.

There is no way in! Tsep declared with a little high squeak of a thought that made Kell smile despite the tension of the moment.

There must be, frio, for Shamra to be taken there.

Yes but maybe that entrance is sealed.

It is certainly not, Fenrir interjected. *Look.*

His fleen-sharp eyes had detected what the others saw a moment later; Slean ships spinning up from amongst the precipitous rocks like flecks of black ash from a fire.

Immediately both great Orbs reacted. The entire landscape moved. In the middle distance, *Skymaster* began to descend and its facets took on the pink-and-green lustre of abalone light as huge energies rose within the craft. Clearly the same thing was happening with *Windhover*.

We must get to our stations, Fenrir declared.

And so they did, and the last glimpse Kell caught was of orbs in their hundreds dropping from *Skymaster* like seeds.

He ran with the wulf along the ship's passageways to one of the chambers where the travel orbs were housed. Many had already departed, taking Magula's war-wulves down to the surface, where they would join with the wyrda and combine in their assault on the city.

There was great busyness here, and yet also a calmness maintained by Skjebne's steady voice that seemed to be made from the air's very molecules; a soft balm of sound.

Feoh was already waiting in the chamber, and Sebalrai joined them a few moments later. She had put on protective leather armour – a back and breast plate and guards for her forearms and shins – and carried two fine knives at her belt, according to Feoh's directions. Feoh now also handed Kell some similar wargear, together with a fully charged fire weapon.

'How are we to travel?' Sebalrai wanted to know. 'In the one orb?'

'I prefer more, for safety.' Skjebne's voice came out of nowhere. 'It is a brutal truth that by following this plan, if one travel orb is destroyed, some of you will live on.'

So Kell, Fenrir and Tsep boarded one vessel, Feoh and Sebalrai another. The wulf and the boy stepped into the warm womb-darkness of the orb, and at once lights bloomed dimly in the cabin, and scattered like stars across the panel of controls. The hatchway closed with a whisper. And then there came the nauseous limbo of falling, which it seemed would go on forever even though but a moment or two passed until the forward viewport opened, surprising Kell with the fact that the orb was already well below the level of the highest peaks, and descending swiftly.

The scape reminded him of the scene above Hugauga; looming cloud layers drifting quickly in the storm-strong

189

winds, now whipping sleet in their faces, now swirling it away to show the pale gleam of light breaking through the overcast; sunshine as thin and tilted as a blade.

And by that meagre light they saw an astonishing spectacle: *Windhover* was drawing back, rising swiftly away as its hull became wrapped around by the strange incandescence that heralded the full surging power of its engines. Meanwhile *Skymaster* fell, swinging down out of the sky in a long low curve that brought it within range of the Slean ships' weaponry. They swarmed about it like ants around fallen fruit, loosing bolt after bolt of glittering energy into the body of the vessel. Incredibly, the orb failed to retaliate; nor did its protective shields engage. And then Kell understood Skjebne's ploy of using *Skymaster* to divert the Slean fleet and draw its fire away from the smaller but more significant orbs raining down into the canyons.

Perhaps Skjebne had been confident that the orb's integral strength could survive such an onslaught. Within moments he was proved wrong. The energy pouring into the orb seemed to reach some critical point: the entire hull began shining dull red like an evening sun: a piece broke away and spun end-over-end trailing banners of smoke. It was the start of a rapid decay. The Slean pilots saw their opportunity and swept in for the final attack through a storm of flame and light.

Kell's heart clenched with grief at the loss of the orb, which in a strange and distant way had been like a friend. Now it was disintegrating swiftly, shedding huge plates of metal as a hundred fires burned across its hull; sinking down below Arcanum's highest peaks that flickered in the glow of the inferno.

Kell watched for as long as he could – forced himself to

watch so that the power of his fury would be fully drawn out. But within seconds the travel orb had plunged into a deep chasm and the vision was whisked from his sight.

And now through the curtains of blizzard the Slean ships hurtled on apace, turning their attention to the lesser orbs. Almost at that instant, Kell saw one collide helplessly with a travel orb, the two vehicles shattering like balls of chalk smashed together, falling in a cascade of sparks. Other Slean vessels picked out their prey with the elegance of hawks and swooped down spitting blue fire . . .

But something wonderful was happening amongst the orbs . . . Even as Kell struggled to understand the change, he realised that the vessels were becoming somehow co-ordinated, moving with the graceful synerthy of the wulfen pack or a flock of birds swept up in the same single thought.

Their own vehicle changed direction with a graceful spin of its drive fields, swinging high and to the right, flying sheer up the grey-black mountain face, tossed like a hurricane leaf under Skjebne's elegant invisible control. Kell lost sight of Sebalrai's orb immediately – it seemed to flicker into shadow and disappear. And then the maps of light on the *bord* alerted him to the fact that their orb was about to suffer a similar fate as it plummeted vertically upwards into shadow, into darkness, into a hidden tunnel drilled through an overhang of rock.

Hugauga was like this, Kell observed. But there was no Radiant Iron here, no Draca, and none of the guiding fields that protected new arrivals. Just once, moving at great speed, the travel orb clipped a rocky spur and went spin-ning, tumbling, whirling insanely carried by its own momentum headlong until the ship's intelligence or Skjebne's guidance righted it and sent it on its way.

His head is filled with the whole scape of the assault, Fenrir said, noticing Kell's thought that Skjebne had not spoken to them for some time. *His mind is guiding every ship, overseeing their every change of direction . . .*

He always did enjoy a game of battleboard.

The quip was intended to lighten the incredible strain of the moment. And yet both wulf and boy realised that the emotion they felt was excitement, of hearts that were light and of blood that was hot with the prospect of combat. Kell looked inside himself and was proud at his lack of fear, at the fire that burned there instead.

They sailed on unchallenged among the labyrinth of tunnels, which sometimes bored through rock and sometimes through ice that was at least as hard as the basalt mountains themselves. And not only tunnels, for periodically they would break out into caverns of varying sizes; occasionally spaces of immense dimensions in which lay ruined the remains of ancient settlements.

These go back to the start of it, Kell said, thinking to himself . . . Or perhaps detecting another's thought, since his mind felt different now . . . it felt no longer alone.

She is with us. Fenrir had noticed it too, that slight but definite change in his mental scape. *It is the Goddess's influence. We are truly within her domain.*

Maybe that is how Skjebne knew which way to bring us; or the eye orbs had already scouted ahead . . .

And so Kell's speculations might have idled on, but for the orb moving beyond the place of the ruins through white and rainbow temples of carven sheet ice into a space deep, deep into the mountains where the All Mother's *gaest* throbbed like a heart in their heads: and at a distance between great hangings of ice there seemed to be raised up a series of galleries linked by broad steps, and there at the top a platform of stone, along which a line of tall figures was walking.

Lyblaeca, Fenrir said, recognising their robes perhaps or knowing through some subtler sense.

There was more to be seen. The travel orb swung round as though to accommodate its passengers' view and Fenrir and Kell were able then to make out a number of Sustren women accompanying the mages as part of the procession; each was dark-robed and some went hooded and some let their faces be seen. All of these were fine-featured and black haired, all ringing a little echo of recognition in Kell's head.

The Goddess favours acolytes that resemble herself. They are all wraiths of Kvasir.

Will they know we are here? That from Tsep, who had by now scrambled up on to Kell's left shoulder.

It is likely . . . Although I do not see any Slean.

Perhaps they are distracted elsewhere by the wyrda and the wulfen.

Skjebne will inform us when he's ready. For now I think we should follow our own good sense.

The orb was able to bring them to the brink of the platform, which by that time was empty. The solemn procession of Sustren and Thrall Brothers had vanished into one of the many tunnels in the rock wall on its far side.

None of them is big enough for the orb –

Then we go on foot. Do you know which tunnel they took Fenrir?

If I did not, I would already be dead, he said wryly, and led them once they had disembarked immediately along one of the passageways that was as featureless as any of the others.

Constantly in Kell's mind hung the thought that this was

a trap; that cleverly the Goddess had separated them off from the main force and would at her own choosing pluck them like fruit from an innocent tree. And it was this impulse of doubt that brought Kell up sharp when they heard the sounds of conflict some distance down a side passage that took them away from the trail.

It is a diversion, Kell. We are meant to follow the Thrall Makers' way.

But our kin are fighting there –

Yes, wulfen, Wyrda . . .

Then I think –

Do not think, Fenrir urged. *Just act.*

Nevertheless Kell drew out his fire weapon and followed the sounds of battle and would not be persuaded otherwise.

I'm glad to see you're wise enough to support my foolishness, Kell said grinning as the wulf loped easily beside him, failing to see the love and loyalty that would have kept Fenrir at the boy's side even into certain death.

The noises grew louder and soon they came upon the scene, emerging into a space that may well have been equal in size to the enclave of Perth, but for the vast hangings of ice, the sheets and spears and pinnacles of ice reaching from the ground right up to the curving paleness of the sky. A sun gleamed somewhere, but its light was so scattered and broken by ice that its position was impossible to determine. And it was a cold sun, for Kell's breath steamed in the air whose sharp touch stung his face as he strained to see into the distance; and then, coming more fully out in the open, realising what was closer at hand . . .

A cadre of six wyrda men with Hora among them was battling with Slean, and to great effect. Although one warrior was downed, his war-kin fought on and a number of the enemy lay twitching on the ground. Further off, eye orbs shoaled unhindered by Slean ships: Kell guessed that the colossal sculptures of ice made it difficult for them to fly. By the same token, there were no travel orbs visible, although they may have been elsewhere on different business.

This is a local skirmish.

But Hora needs our help. He is injured remember –

Kell, Shamra is not down there!

Then restraining his impulsiveness at last, Kell nodded and made to turn his back on the fray.

And a Slean soldier, fully armoured, raced towards him from his hiding place nearby.

Fenrir spun around snarling, but had no time to leap. The Slean's steel fist lashed out and sent the wulf reeling, and that same fist swung back and smashed into the side of Kell's skull.

Stars exploded and ice-gleams flew through his head, each accompanied by dazzling pain. But Kell's thoughts seemed to be clear. He would jump up and lunge within the enemy's defences and drive a blade through his chest –

His legs would not move; his arms would not obey him. He was a cloth doll dropped by a child and forgotten. Fenrir tried to shake the dizziness out of his brain and relaunch his attack. And even valiant Tsep struggled free and stood on Kell's chest shrieking with fury and the hurt of the light.

And then Kell started to dream, or believed that he had. A rippling appeared in the air between himself and the Slean soldier, and the warrior hesitated momentarily.

A scoremark streaked across his armour, and an instant later another, deeper, which penetrated the metal. The

Slean backstepped one pace, two – threw up his hands protectively –

And his head leaped from his shoulders, and even before the body toppled forward the air had thickened and swirled into colour and form, and Feoh stood looking disapprovingly down at Kell, with Sebalrai standing beside her.

'Skjebne,' she said, 'is very angry with you.'

She helped him up and smoothed her hand across his temple and the hammering subsided.

'He is guiding all of us. You were meant to follow the lyblaeca, as we were but by a different route.'

'At least you're safe.' Sebalrai addressed Kell but would not look at him.

'For the moment anyway. Have we suffered many losses?'

'A few of the wyrda are slain, some injured. Thorbyorg is withdrawing the wounded instantly from battle: they are being taken to a redoubt closer to the surface for now.'

Kell nodded and surveyed the scuffle below. The last of the Slean were being dispatched and Hora, bloodied from his kills but also from his own unmended wound, raised a hand to let his friends know that the fighting was over.

'He will make his own way,' Feoh said, sweeping like a bird through his mind. The wyrda and the orbs, where they are able to fly, will take the brunt of the Slean assault. We must reach the place of Gebedraedan before the ritual is finished.'

'But the All Mother will know – she will be in our heads and see us coming!'

'Skjebne's tactics will keep the Slean busy,' Feoh said, moving quickly now towards Kell's original path. 'And besides, the Goddess has her mind on other things . . .'

★

It was impossible to find Creation's smallest particle, or to hold all-there-was before the eye. That was her thought as she waited for the final energies to be assembled. Patience would not be the right word to describe the feeling that simmered inside her. There was no word. Perhaps the closest comparison was the anticipation a little girl might feel on being let out of her house for the first time alone on a spring morning, ready to walk into the world.

And Kvasir remembered how that had been, and an immense sadness welled up inside her at what she had done.

But there would be no wavering now, no doubt. Only going forward. The world was waking and the prospect of further imprisonment had become unbearable. Whenever she considered it her mind trembled on the brink, fearful of the instant of falling. Even taking this child's life was a price worth paying to be free of that immeasurable horror.

She was everywhere; some splinter of her ancient personality in every fragment of weorthan that existed throughout the world. But the essence, here, now, was focused in this single chamber, watching these sorcerers go about their spellbinding work.

Kvasir let her attention become very still and settled on the girl who hung immobile in the crystal egg.

She was beautiful – as beautiful as Kvasir had been, yet not as beautiful as she had become in womanhood when, at the peak of her brilliance and poised on the edge of even greater achievements, the World Directorate had summoned her and her team of technicians and elaborated their plan.

At that time – so very long ago – it had been a vision

filled with bravado and wonder and the glory of noble sacrifice. Besides, and more selfishly, Kvasir relished the prospect of immortal time in which to learn, to soak up the knowledge of the world, to know what the future would bring. And of course the honour of being given such immense responsibility was indescribable.

A number of Kvasir's colleagues possessed equal abilities, but only she came forward and offered herself to the task. Those others, those little meaningless specks of flesh, did not have the strength within them . . .

The All Mother smiled inside and reined-in her thoughts. Did it matter now what the nameless forgotten dead chose or chose not to do? Indeed, Kvasir herself barely remembered anything about that time or about the transformation that she had undergone. She recalled standing naked in a room, and then of lying in an operating theatre while surgeons worked around her and attendant machines drifted through the air with a gentle humming of energy fields. She remembered a tunnel of light, and beyond that light was a world of weorthan, into which she had first emerged, before her essential consciousness moved on to Arcanum . . .

Years, possibly centuries had gone by, and the World Directorate and her co-workers at the Institute and her friends and what family she'd loved were now dust. Gradually she came to understand that the missing time had been a period of intense *self-absorption*, a kind of reverie when she had assimilated the incalculable amount of data needed to enable humanity to survive. And it became a constant flow as her remote points of presence monitored the encroaching Ice and life within the enclaves.

That had formed the pattern of things for many

generations. But the Wintering was relentless, the cold intense. Far-flung terminals had malfunctioned: communication with entire communities was cut off and isolated populations were left to fend for themselves. The ones that remained under her influence were guided by a gentle hand, and sometimes not so gentle if the fabric of their civilization threatened to unravel. Occasionally in the long history of her reign it had become necessary for the Goddess to intervene more completely in the affairs of men. Three times she had deliberately allowed a corrupt community to perish, shutting off their power so that the people died in the cold and the all-consuming dark. And elsewhere she had shaped society radically according to her will; for men should never be allowed simply to turn their backs on the world that nurtured them and stumble out on to the Ice, there to be cut down and become nothing under the uncaring sky.

So she had woven terror-tales, the Mythologies to keep societies stable and respectful of the Ice – and, she admitted it now, respectful of herself. Wasn't that the very least she should be granted in return for her sacrifice to this endless desolation of being so alone!

But human beings are as fickle as they are ephemeral: and through stupidity or a subversiveness that runs in the blood, they are tempted away from the given truths in search of their own reality. They are never satisfied, always searching. And once the temple of belief starts to crumble, people cannot be stopped until they have built another from their own chosen stones.

So it was that Kvasir's thoughts turned to an ending of her charge, to be free of it at long, long last. She had watched with amusement, and then with intense interest and admiration, as the Thrall Makers of Kairos had rediscovered some of the old secrets of life and, in various ways, infused dead substance with its spark. But the creation of the Slean had been something different again – the forging of a quasi life whose span was vast barring accident and injury. Slean flesh did not bleed or age; it was artful enough in itself to take the mould of every natural cell, maintaining its original function and form. And through further trials, aided by the Sustren and the All Mother's immense resource of knowledge, the lyblaeca – the Masters of the Thrall – discovered how they might distill the spirit of Kvasir into a body that had been so tempered . . .

And she looked again upon her future self and yearned to feel herself contained within its bounds, and to breathe the world's sweet air and hear its songs and to know that the words of her story had not been written on water.

Kell could feel the forces of their attack gathering up around him. Skjebne with Thorbyorg's skill had deployed the wyrda cleverly; groups of men were hacking their way with devastating effect through the dwindling opposition the Slean threw up against them. There were surprisingly few of them, and of the hyrnetu there was no sign at all. It occurred to Kell that the All Mother had only a token force to protect her, its power spent in trying to prevent this final attack.

The party saw one other skirmish; two wyrda, each com-manding an armoured boar, making an end of three Slean minions who had not possessed the wit to retreat. Brutally, the warriors had given the boars free rein and the *eofor* were now wreaking terrible damage on the downed foe.

They hurried on. Kell grew aware of wulfen gathering nearby, streaking like spirits through the ice tunnels towards the same goal.

'Almost there. Shamra is just up ahead,' Feoh said aloud for the benefit of Sebalrai and the eye orb that had just then joined them. No Slean barred their way: no hyrnetu sprang from niches in the rock to delay them – all had now been destroyed, or else were dispersed too far across Arcanum to be of help. Kell and Feoh, Sebalrai and Fenrir and Tsep burst into the cavern of Gebedraedan and there put an end to a dream.

Shamra seemed to be awake. Trapped in the crystal shell, her eyes followed the progress of the figures that now dashed into the chamber. There was instant chaos among the lyblaeca and the Sustren who attended them. One Thrall Brother snapped out a string of ciphered words that was curse and spell and an exclamation of surprise all in one. And the fair-haired boy with a war-proud yell pounced upon the mage and smashed him to the ground in his fury.

Hadn't these people been warned? Kell wondered now within his own mind. Hadn't they seen their enemy coming? The Thrall Maker crumpled easily and put up no resistance – But the Sustren whirled and spat like wildcats and lashed with silver claws that had been grafted into their fingers. Tsep fluttered ahead with little high cheeping sounds and dived into one Sister's robes. Immediately she began a ludicrous panic dance and stumbled away screeching.

Two Thrall Makers, acting together, hurled up a barrier of light. Fenrir in mid-leap was caught within its veils and his body blazed like lightning and sparks crackled from the tip of every strand of fur. He howled and was thrown aside.

But now Magula and Wulfmaer and the other pack fighters arrived and added to the rout. There would be no stopping them, and no mage or Sister stood in her way as Feoh approached the crystal egg, a weapon in her hand, and lifted her arm up high.

Kell's senses ceased to race. The mad battle-rage inside him subsided and again he felt the nearness of the All Mother . . . And noticed now that a large part of the cavern was composed of translucent ice locked within the honeycomb rock . . . But not ice – something more marvellous and infinitely more dangerous – a sea's vastness held back by restraining fields.

And as the god-given understanding struck him, the water surged out and assumed a human shape, wrapped its arms around him and drew him down into the depths.

12

The Memory Of Water

Kell had never been the most powerful of swimmers, and for a little while he floundered helplessly, struggling inside a diamond, until he realised that he could breathe, caught as he was in a bubble of air.

He realised too that he was not alone.

So Kvasir, will you kill me now?

I wanted to look upon you closely, Kell. You have come up like a seedling from the soil, to flourish here and deny me my life. Of course I will kill you.

No one denies you life, Kvasir, only your action of taking it freely when it is not yours to take.

And how many lives have you taken Kell, since you first left the enclave of Perth? . . . There was a pause, and then a sigh that seemed to shiver through the ocean.

They have released Shamra from the weorthan shell. She is beyond me now. I have lost her.

Where are you?

I am everywhere you look. Oh, the ancient technicians were clever. They understood the limits of crystal. They worked out how the original impulse of all life arose in the seas . . . The rain remembers, Kell. The world weeps for itself . . .

Kell found he had limited movement, and looked about

himself and saw the trembling light of the cavern of Gebedraedan and other chambers further off.

You cannot reach them.

Don't kill them too, Kell pleaded. *They are my friends.*

Perhaps I choose to kill them because they are your friends.

Kell knew it would be futile to try to buy time. He had nothing to trade, and the All Mother's purpose was set. Driven by bitterness and regret and an envy of the simple act of being alive, she was in the end a false and cruel god. She would grant no mercy to him now.

Kell guessed what she would do. Or perchance it was a terrible premonition. Either way, he had one chance to stop her.

Almost without thinking, for the *cristilla* thought for itself, he delved in his tunic and found the stone that Feoh had given him and fumbled it out from its pouch.

Perhaps Kvasir, for all her incredible knowledge, had never seen the gemstone before or its like, for her mind was empty of suspicion. Or perhaps she was cleverer and more than Kell had imagined, and now the wish for oblivion was upon her . . . He lifted the jewel up in his palm and had time to admire it briefly –

All eras end –

And whether those were his words or Kvasir's mattered not at all to the soul of the crystal that knew now its own time had come.

Kell saw nothing of it, for his eyes were burned blind in that instant. He was aware of a light shining with all the power of the sun, which did not fade but blazed up and blazed up in a cleansing wash of brilliance throughout the subterranean sea. And the Goddess was made to forget herself, and her waters broke and a dreadful pressure squeezed Kell's body and a thunderous roar sounded in his brain.

Though he guessed he was dying he felt a wonderful release as something much greater than the Goddess – perhaps Wierd itself, the Nurturer – took him up and swathed him in darkness and warmth, and rocked him like a child gently onward, onward on his journey . . .

Skjebne's full attention was contained in a single thought. The eye orbs, swarming through the caverns of Arcanum, had come upon the living waters at its heart; and he had known the sea's purpose and its name. For thousands of years the ligetu drawn from the core of the world had maintained it in stasis, giving the All Mother the illusion of life once Kvasir's final heartbeat had ended.

Skjebne recognised the miracle of that place, and its awful danger. His first attempts to send orbs into the ocean had met with defeat. The same fields that contained the body of water kept the craft out.

So, from a distance, he watched events unfold, meanwhile deploying all of *Windhover*'s remaining travel orbs – some to collect the wyrda who were still scouring the tunnels and chambers of Arcanum, some to wait just beyond the chamber of Gebedraedan until the time came to act.

That moment arrived unexpectedly.

There was an immense flash, a release of energy that radiated to the outermost limits of the All Mother's mind. Its effects were instantaneous, though Skjebne wondered if they could ever be complete; purging thought and understanding from the atoms of the water, allowing the Goddess to disremember herself and all that she had ever been or intended. Alderamin had once told him something of the stone, the jewel of purification. He had seen one similar used on a gang of men whose crimes had been heinous, and whose correction was the bliss of absolute release. They had become as oblivious as the trees, alive to the world but with all their self-intelligence gone, innocents without a dark idea between them. And even now Skjebne could not decide if the jewel was a punishment or a forgiveness.

He had been able to transmit a partial last-moment warning to the others in the chamber of Gebedraedan and began to send the travel orbs to positions as close to them as possible. As the Goddess's memory faded, so the restraining fields died and the sea crashed in.

Feoh, Fenrir, Sebalrai – they would all have to fend for themselves. The greatest peril was to Kell. The air pocket around him had vanished and the sea had folded him in its depths, drawing him quite quickly now towards one of the gigantic ducts that led outside to the ocean. And Skjebne saw that maelstrom: from the viewpoint of a single eye orb poised above the cliffs, he watched half the rock face torn away by the unimaginable pressure of water that burst out in a vast gushing cascade of white chaos.

Meanwhile the travel orb plummeted down. Its light blazed on and there ahead the boy hung in a huge green dark, arms spread out as though in grotesque mimicry of greeting. Skjebne spun the vehicle round and risked all by releasing the door seals; dropping the hatch and scooping Kell up; then activating the orb's system of pumps and vents to clear the flood before he drowned – knowing that he might already be dead, extinguished one way or another by the All Mother's wrath.

Skjebne sent the ship upward against the water's weight,

clearing the surface moments later in a fountain of spray, while the sea below churned, a frenzy of whirlpools, and sank and sank away abandoning its ancient bed.

Soon what had been the shore became a shelf of rock overhung by great sheets of ice in an immense globed cavern. The orb settled here, its energies fading: the hatch folded down and presently ligetu lights flared in the darkness and a bedraggled grey wulf and a tall dark-haired woman came into view.

Kell saw with different eyes now. He looked upon himself from a few spans away and did not condemn the boy who sat there shivering in his blankets. Mighty Hora wept nearby for the death of his comrades and their eofor. Magula's head hung low in remembrance of Wulfmaer and Eodor, Gauda and Rof. But the *maegenwulf* was only quiescent, and the pack would know strength and life and the wild places again.

Feoh walked over and put her palm to Kell's brow. He lifted his head and smiled and could not see her through the white quartz of his own eyes. Using Fenrir's vision instead, Kell thought he looked rather stupid grinning upward like that with a man-bat perched on his shoulder.

'There is no pain from the blinding. Just other hurts.'

The company was camped on a plateau close to the surface of the ground. Blizzard winds whipped above and howled and whistled through the tunnels and voids of Arcanum. It was a dead place now, but for these survivors circled around a score of fires scattering into the distance. Wulfen and wyrda guarded those Sustren and lyblaeca that had lived, their destiny yet to be decided. But the few Slean Thorbyorg's men encountered had been promptly slain.

'There is much work to do here,' Feoh said. The eye orbs scattering afar were still discovering new chambers filled with weorthan and complex machineries. 'Much work', she added, 'of understanding. What will you do, Skjebne?'

He had recently joined them, having secured *Windhover* after examining *Skymaster*'s ruin. His once-wounded hip was now fully healed, and he walked with a sprightly step over to the fire, prodded it with a stick and watched the sparks rise spiralling upward. He seemed in a mellow and reflective mood.

'Well, I may spend some seasons here learning more of Arcanum and the Wintering's course. I think there are very valuable secrets to be found. Beyond that —' He smiled and the firelight gleamed on his forehead and sparkled in his eyes. 'Beyond that I intend to travel the Sun's Way and witness other worlds — if Thorbyorg and the wyrda will be patient and wait until my duties here are completed.'

Hora wiped his eyes and lifted the juggon of *meodu* that rested beside him and took a long guzzle. 'I suppose the First Eolder might be persuaded. And I suppose', he said grumpily, 'I ought to stay with you. Someone needs to anchor that impulsiveness of yours. And Feoh?'

'Well, my inclination is to remain with the Sustren. There are many women here who are powerful healers, and that healing will be needed all across the world. But with the Goddess gone the Sisters must reflect on their purpose and make their intention clear. Perhaps I can tempt them to Hugauga. It is a secure place and' — the ghost of a smile — 'and Wrynn is there.'

'I want to go with you, Feoh,' said Shamra, speaking up for the first time. She looked much older than Skjebne remembered her: six seasons ago a young girl was taken from the village of the Shore People, and a woman had been found here today. What she had endured at the All Mother's hands might never be known unless Shamra herself chose to speak of it. But her experiences would have been profound, and she was much changed. For all the horror, her words sounded sure and determined.

'I want to go with you,' she repeated, and looked to Feoh and Skjebne and Hora her original companions, not for approval but to know they understood that her mind was set.

Fenrir's eyes watched the girl move across to Kell and sit beside him. She held his hands.

'I wouldn't want to hurt you any more than you have suffered in searching me out. But Wierd has changed us, Kell. I do not think a little house by a pretty river, with a few children perhaps and a paddock of *gats* and *sceap* will suit either of us now. I want to learn the Sisters' ways, and be a healer like Feoh.'

She leant and kissed Kell's blind eyes and then, just once, his lips.

'You know your road, as I know mine. Wierd has not changed us, Shamra, it has made us more truly who we are. That is right as it should be. But we will meet from time to time and share a tale or two.'

Shamra moved away and Sebalrai, full of so many feelings that she hardly trusted her voice, came and knelt at Kell's side and spoke without looking at him directly.

'What of you Kell? What is it in your heart to do now?'

And it felt to Kell then that the doorway to one great adventure had closed but that other lands lay spread out before him. There would be joy, he was sure, and many tears; and through it all he could only be his first true self, just a man ploughing a furrow.

The World Of The Wintering
GLOSSARY

Aethgar – One of Alderamin's soldiers, killed in the last battle of Edgetown.

Aglaeca – Monster.

Alderamin – Alderamin is the amber merchant Kell and his friends meet in *Ice*.

Alef (and Thoba and Myrgen) – Three Wyrda companions who accompany Kell and his friends to Thule to destroy Helcyrian and the Shahini Tarazad.

All Mother – Aka the Goddess and Little Sister. The All Mother is the controlling force in Perth, an apparently omnipotent presence who maintains the world of the enclave at all levels, from the environment to the spiritual structure of the Community. Kell and his friends finally discover that Little Sister (like Orwell's Big Brother) is an intelligent construction that exists planet-wide – but it is flawed and fragmented, both in terms of its physical interconnectedness and the ghost of the neurotic/paranoid personality that lies at its heart. The All Mother represents the smothering mother archetype, the Earth Mother, and the 'mystification of technology' that afflicts the general populace.

Amber – A fossilised resin which quite often contains the perfectly preserved remains of plants, insects, even small lizards. In the Wintering it represents preservation through imprisonment, a state that exists also in Perth.

Anwealda – Ruler.

Aquizi – One of Kell's tutors, whom Kell despises for his arrogance yet fears because of his cruelly-applied power.

Aurok – A huge bull-like herbivore, sacrificed by the Wulfen so that they can talk with their deity, the Godwulf. An aurok must be defeated in one-to-one battle for this to occur.

Awyrcancoin – Payment for labour.

Bealdor – A leader in war.

Bearn – Child.

Beorc – The leader of one of Kano's escapee groups. His name means birth or regeneration.

Birca – Birca is one of Kano's rebel band. He did not survive the escape from Perth. His name signifies growth, but is used in a darkly ironic way when set within the false paradise of the enclave.

Bismarian Wall – The Wall of Shame in Thule on which Helcyrian's prisoners are caged.

Bord – Table.

Broken Place – Another name for Thule, an enclave which is also broken in a psychological sense, ruled as it is by the psychotic tyrant Helcyrian.

Brooor – Brother.

Ceorl – Peasants.

Chertan – Leader of a bandit pack whom Kell and his friends encounter on their journey East.

Ciepemann – A trader.

Community – The name by which the population of Perth is known. It is used ironically throughout.

Compound words – Appear throughout the story; heartbonded, honeygrass, lantern-apple, elderman, meltstone and others. Apart from being a stylistic device, such compounded words create links with the linguistic structure of the Anglo-Saxon culture which provided a model for the culture Kell and his friends meet through Alderamin.

Corvus – Wulfen word for crow.

Cristilla – Generally, a crystal or gemstone. In Thaw the word refers to a powerful weapon of radiance which Feoh passes on to Kell, having received it previously as a gift from Alderamin.

Dispossessed – The dispossessed are those members of the populace who, like Kano, have removed the weorthan glass from their eyes (see Weorthan).

Dreamhoard – The mass of weorthan crystal below Thule containing the vast knowledge of the world. But the knowledge, like the 'Hoard itself, is fractured and incomplete.

Drengs – Biomechanical minions of Helcyrian. Drengs

are once-human beings shackled more or less completely to artificial components.

Drycraeft – Magic or enchantment (or, from our perspective, sophisticated technological processes or effects).

Drycraeftig – Magically skilled.

Dweorg – A dwarf, one of the Brising or Shining Ones. The Brising traditionally reside in Kairos: they are metal workers of great skill.

Ealdbeorn – An older brother in terms of friendship and wisdom rather than blood links.

Ealdmodor – 'Old Mother', ususually used as an insult. Pl: ealdmodoren.

Eardstapa – Travelling merchants.

Eargnewulf – A Tarazad word meaning 'the miserable (wulf)'.

Edgetown – The trader settlement ruled by Alderamin. Edgetown represents a frontier; it is a fledgling community eventually wiped out by the Shahini Tarazad who come from Thule in the Barbaric Lands.

Elhaz – A Wyrda warrior killed in Thule.

Enclave – An enclosed environment within which communities live in isolation protected from the global ice. The enclave of Perth is a hollowed-out mountain.

Enjeck – Husband of Munin. They were Kell's last temporary family before he left Perth.

Eodor – A young wulf in Magula's pack. Also a word meaning 'protector'.

Eofor – Boar.

Eoldermen – The elders of a group.

Erulian – An esoteric group (some believe they are a distinct breed) of Thrall Makers or enchanters. From what can be gleaned of their powers, it appears that the Erulian use a combination of innate mental abilities and technological devices to affect the fabric of reality. It is said that they among few mortal creatures can change the way that Wierd is woven.

Eye Of The Rad – A mysterious room near Uthgaroar. Made of a strange translucent substance, the room creates the viewpoint of one standing in the centre of the heavens. This signifies the purpose of the Sigel Rad and the destiny of the Wyrda Craeftum.

Faeder – Father.

Faedera – The pack leader before Magula.

Faellanstan – The Tumblestones, a high pass lying to the north-east of Edgetown.

Faest – Secretly.

Fenrir – One of Magula's pack and a young wulf touched by Wierd. Fenrir or his offspring are fated to drive humankin from the world and fill the sky with blood. The symbolism of this prophecy is unclear.

Feoh – Feoh is a powerful telepath and healer. She is one of Kano's rebel group and is heartbonded to him. After

Kano's death and Shamra's mysterious capture, Feoh goes in search of her and becomes initiated into the Sustren. Feoh's name is linked with fulfilment, well being and nourishment.

Ferhocraeft – 'Mind craft'; the process of creative thought and the products of that thought which in the past has been called Teknology.

Forraedan – One of the Thrall Makers of Kairos, and a lyblaeca or master mage.

Frea – Master, as in 'sir'.

Frio – Friend.

Furhwudu – Fir trees.

Furrow – A furrow is one symbol of Kell's life. It implies predetermination and the illusion of choice. See Wierd.

Fwthark – Hora's friend and a fellow Wyrda warrior. Fwthark dies during the fall of Thule. His name means unity.

Gaeleran – A teacher.

Gaest – The soul or spirit of an object or place.

Garulf – Genera (pl: generan), or assistant, to Thorbyorg.

Gast – A night spirit, any ghostly thing.

Gat – A mountain goat.

Gauda – A wulf in Magula's pack.

Gebedraedan – A dangerous and powerful ritual performed by the Lyblaeca in which bio-formative fields are activated and modified to create subgenetic changes in individuals or an entire species. The Seetus, Wulfen and Hreaomus were all created in this way. Latterly the ceremony has been corrupted to produce the Slean.

Gebrooor – True Brother. This is a term of great affection and respect.

Gedrhyt – Band or company of people.

Gefera – A wulfen word for companion.

Gegilda – A guild member.

Gesittan – A command to be still and calm.

Gifu – Gifu is the landsman who trained Kell in his craft. He represents 'ignorance is bliss', perfect Zen. Gifu never questions what's around him. He observes the rhythms of the world and draws a deep pleasure from nature. He has lived and will die like an ear of the wheat that he cultivates. The name Gifu (also Gyfu) is a runic word meaning a gift.

Glass – Glass has a special significance in Kell's world. The glass of Skjebne's farscope opens up the horizons, but usually glass has a sinister aspect linked with the controlling influence of the All Mother. Every child of Perth is given an oyster-shaped chunk of glass in infancy. It is tuned to the innocent's mind. It whispers to him, reinforces the Mythologies, and allows the Goddess to know his actions, words, and even perhaps his thoughts. Kell and Shamra's destruction of their oyster glass after meeting Kano is a profoundly symbolic and empowering act. Glass is also crafted into subtle lenses or pellicles which are placed over the eyes of babies to filter their reality. Kano allowed Kell to see the truth of things by plucking out his lenses.

Godwulf – The one deity of the Wulfen. The Godwulf is composed of the souls of all dead Wulfen, and is a day-to-day part of the existence of all that are alive. The Godwulf is the past and the destiny of the species, expressing itself most powerfully in the here-and-now.

Guardian helmet – Headgear which allows the wearer simultaneous control of all the Orbs of the Wyrda Craeftum.

Hacele – A cloak.

Hagen – One of Alderamin's kinsmen.

Healm – A mat.

Heartbonding – Couples are predestined to live together in adulthood and produce offspring. It is of course the All Mother who decides which boy and girl shall be introduced as children. From that point on they are required to meet socially until the time comes when they are officially bonded. Their children are soon taken away from them, however, to have their minds moulded at the Tutorium. From there they live with a succession of temporary families until they are old enough to be independent.

Helcyrian – Dictatorial ruler of Thule. One of the Sustren, she maintains an iron control over the drengs of the Shahini Tarazad.

Heoden – A wulf in Magula's pack.

Heorot – A wulfen word for deer.

Heorrenda – An armoured boar of the Wyrda Craeftum. He is put under Hora's care.

Hora – One of Kano's rebel group. Hora was a fisherman who later joins a mercenary warrior band known as the Wyrda Craeftum. It is through Hora's contacts with the Wyrda that Kell and his friends find the means to explore the outer world.

Hreaomus – A species of man-bat that Kell and his friends encounter at the plateau of the orbs.

Hrothwulf – The oldest wulf in Magula's pack.

Hugauga – A large settlement on the Plain of Thurisaz (Gateway) where Kell and his friends meet with the Thrall Maker Wrynn.

Hwaet! – Meaning 'Greetings' or 'Listen!'

Hyld – A wulf in Magula's pack.

Hyrdefolk – Tenders of cattle and sheep.

Hyrnetu – Literally 'hornets' or insects. The hyrnetu are mechanical servo-devices which have evolved into the slave-weapons of the Slean, who in turn serve the Lyblaeca – indeed, some of the Thrall Makers themselves have undergone the process of becoming Slean.

Ice Demon – The Ice Demon symbolises the harshness and destructiveness of the world beyond the enclave. It is the bogeyman invoked to frighten children and adults alike. Kell's encounter with the Demon at the conclusion of *Ice* marks an important step in his rite of passage to adulthood and independence.

Jadhma – One of Alderamin's wives, and birth-mother of Shaula.

Kairos – Kairos has been called the City Out Of Time. It is a strange and enigmatic place, as though built on a gateway between worlds, curiously unaffected by climate or circumstances. It is the home of the Erulian, the Thrall Makers whom the Sustren believe can make the dreams of weorthan a living reality.

Kano – Leader of the rebel movement in Perth. Kano's power lies in his ability to see things as they are in the enclave (and there is a technological explanation behind this), coupled with his vast anger that the people should be made to live under an illusion. It is that anger which makes Kano's life burn briefly but bright as the sun. He dies in battle with the Ice Demon at Thule. His name is a runic word signifying an opening up, renewed clarity and a dispelling of the darkness.

Kell – Kell is the archetypal adolescent caught between innocence and experience. His world is uncomplicated in itself (so he thinks), and his life as a ploughboy is simple but for the questions that trouble him greatly and which eventually lead to his escape from Perth. Like all of the inhabitants of the enclave, Kell has no family name.

Lesath – An old friend of Alderamin's, slaughtered horribly years before in the Dawn Mountains.

Ligetu – A mysterious flameless energy used for light and heat.

Loefsonu – One of the eoldermen of Uthgaroar. Leofsonu

represents the wish to maintain the status quo, and is very resistant to Kell's ideas for change.

Luparo – The Wulf Slaughterer, a mythical being personifying the nemesis of the Wulfen.

Lyblaeca – The most experienced members of the guild of the Thrall Makers, seduced by the Sustren in *Thaw* into furthering the All Mother's plans.

Maegenwulf – The strength of the pack, in all senses of the word.

Magula – The leader of the wulfen pack Kell encounters at the end of his imprisonment in Thule.

Meodu – Honeyed liquor.

Mirach – Nurse to Alderamin's children. She is slain in the forest by Tarazad drengs.

Modor – Mother.

Mox – 'Mechanical ox'. The mox represents the blending of biology and technology which reached its peak just before the onset of the Ice. The early mention of the mox is a precursor to Kell's realisation that electronic implantation has gone way beyond the control of beasts.

Munin – Wife of Enjeck. They were Kell's last temporary family before he left Perth.

Mwl – A strong horse-like pack animal.

Myrgen – See Alef.

Mythologies – The body of knowledge that every member of the Community is taught as gospel. The

Mythologies serve to perpetuate the influence of the All Mother by creating a deep dread of all that supposedly lies outside the enclave. By doubting the truth of the Mythologies, Kell suffers increasingly severe punishments inflicted by the All Mother and the educational system she maintains.

Odal – The main city which lies at the centre of Perth, close to the Central Lake. Odal is the commercial and, so the population supposes, the industrial centre of Perth. No-one bothers to question where new moxen and other animals come from, nor the vehicles which always seem to be in plentiful supply. Kell discovers that a huge industrial complex seems to run automatically behind the façade of the enclave. The word Odal means 'home'.

Onweardnes – The spirit or essence of a thing.

Opticus – See Sky gleams.

Orbs – Faceted metal orbs of various sizes are inextricably linked to the tribe of the Wyrda Craeftum and their destiny known as the Sigel Rad. Small orbs (somewhat larger than a human head) are free-floating and can transmit distant images to the Wyrda. Kell and his friends eventually discover huge globes of similar construction. These are vehicles capable of astonishingly swift travel. All of the orbs are somehow connected to the largely unknown workings of the Universal Wheel.

Othila – This is the village where Kell lives and was raised. The name comes from a rune signifying separation.

Perth – The enclave in which Kell lives. It is an enclosed and totalitarian world, controlled completely (we assume at first) by the All Mother. Perth or Peorth is also one of the 'basic runes' signifying a pot, a container, the womb.

Praeceptor – The head tutor at the Tutorium. His word is traditionally accepted and followed unquestioningly.

Rad – The leader of one of Kano's escapee groups. His name means movement and direction.

Rof – A wulf in Magula's pack.

Saeferth – One of Alderamin's kinsmen.

Sceatt – A gold coin of relatively little value.

Sealt – A savoury nut.

Sebalrai – A young girl whom Feoh rescued from Chertan and his crew of bandits. Sebalrai's rare mental gift acts upon the mind to make her imperceptible. As she develops this power she is able to include others within her area of influence. Although Shamra is Kell's heartbonded, Sebalrai comes to have a special place in his affections.

Seetus – The 'Zen whale', the last great whale of the oceans. Seetus is a semi-mystical being who understands very clearly the relationship between mind and matter and the illusion of the perceived world. Seetus seems able to manipulate matter itself by changing the matrix of space-and-time within which physical objects have their ex-istence.

Setl – A couch.

Shahini Tarazad – The swarm-like tribe of soldier minions ruled absolutely by Helcyrian.

Shamra – Shamra is Kell's 'heartbonded', his chosen mate. She has to undergo a special teaching to develop her outstanding telepathic abilities. Before she escapes from Perth with Kell, Shamra's destiny was to have been an academic at the Tutorium. Subsequently she is captured and initiated into the Sustren, a mystical group consisting only of women. Their purpose is connected intimately with the enhanced mental powers that some people possess, and the occult technology of which Little Sister is a part.

Shaula – Youngest daughter of Alderamin the trader. Years before, Shaula was traumatised by a creature that attacked her camp and slaughtered her father's old friend Lesath.

Shore People – A community led by Faras, whom Kell and his friends encounter after escaping from Perth. The shore people display onemindedness to a high degree: they act as one individual. Furthermore, their genetic structure is changing generation by generation. Soon they will have evolved into ocean-dwelling creatures and will leave the land forever. Their deity, or at least their guide, is Seetus the last great whale.

Sigel Rad – The Sun's Way. It is the ancient Wierd of the Wyrda Craeftum to journey to the sky along this sacred path.

Skjebne – One of Kano's fellow rebels and, eventually, a mentor and close friend to Kell, who delights in and respects the man's boundless curiosity and vast fund of knowledge.

Sky gleams – These are the mysterious lights which drift and swarm across the sky every night in Perth, after the sun has 'ungathered'. Virtually all inhabitants of the Community fear the dark and so very few of them ever witness the spectacle of the sky gleams. Kell goes out of his way to watch them. At first he carries the general belief that they are mysterious elemental beings, or maybe the thoughts of the All Mother herself. Only gradually does he realise that the gleams form part of a sophisticated surveillance system, which Kano calls the opticus.

Skymaster – The first of the Great Orbs of the Wyrda Craeftum to be discovered by Kell and his friends. Others include Cloudfarer, Heavenwalker and Windhover. The human race has a long history of naming important vehicles!

Slean – Literally 'Shadow-Slayers', referring to the notion that a man gives up his humanity (his shadow) to become immortal through the process and ritual of Gebedraedan. Slean flesh is greyish and does not bleed, though it can be damaged beyond the point at which a creature can sustain its quasi-life.

Snaka – Snakes or serpents.

Spedigfeolc – 'Wealthy ones'.

Straetfolc – 'Street folk', the common people.

Sustren – A mystical female group also known as the Sisterhood. Their allegiance lies with the entity expressed through the All Mother in Perth (and in various other guises across the world). The Sustren train their initiates in diverse mental arts of an occult nature. Their purpose seemingly is to incarnate their goddess on Earth.

Sweorian – Be calm.

Swoestor – Sister; a term of endearment.

Synerthy – Thinking-together-all-as-one. This ability, inherent in the Shore Folk and some wulfen packs, confers great power upon the group in whatever they do, from communicating to hunting to prayer.

Thoba – See Alef.

Thorbyorg – The First Eolder of Uthgaroar and leader of the Wyrda Craeftum.

Thrall Makers – Another name for the Erulian, a breed of enchanters who supposedly possess the ability to affect the weave of fate and realise the heart's deepest dreams.

Thule – A dark and mysterious enclave east of Edgetown. It is ruled by Helcyrian, an insane and corrupted dictator.

Tir – An elder wulf in Magula's pack.

Traveller – A semi-sentient vehicle that Kano and his group use to escape from Perth. Alderamin and the people Outside also call them ice-wains.

Tsep – One of the Hreaomus horde who stows aboard Skymaster and befriends Kell and his companions.

Tyr – A young girl terrified by the darkening of Perth. Her name represents the female quality.

Universal Wheel – The central symbol of the Wyrda Craeftum. The actual Universal Wheel is a device which is in contact with and somehow controls all of the orbs possessed by the Wyrda or spoken about in their legends.

The Wheel seems to act beyond the boundaries of time and space that mark out the human world.

Unsynnig – Untainted, innocent.

Utewulfen – The 'out wulves', the outrunners of a pack on the move.

Uthgaroar – The ancient mountain home of the Wyrda Craeftum, sacred because of the presence of the Eye of the Rad on a nearby mountaintop.

Verres – A genetically modified armoured boar owned by Zauraq of the Wyrda Craeftum.

Waere – A guard at Edgetown.

Wayd – One of Alderamin's soldiers, killed in the last battle of Edgetown.

Weorthan – This word, from the language of the Wyrda Craeftum and other peoples of the outer world, means 'to be' or 'to become'. It is linked with the notion of destiny or Wierd.

Wierd – This word is of central importance to Kell's life and the world of the Wintering. Its subtle aspects include destiny, 'what will be will be', yet also 'that which is to happen', Wierd (nothing to do with weird) implies the flexibility to act within a framework constructed by higher powers. As Hora might say, Wierd is like a game of cards. The hand you are dealt is your predestiny, but how you play those cards is your free will in life. Wierd is linked with weorthan and with Wyrda, 'the fates'.

Wildedeor – A wulfen word meaning wild and led only

by instinct. Used often to describe wulfen packs who lack reflective thought and the gift of onemindedness.

Winsael – A wine drinking hall or tavern.

Wintering – The period, measuring some tens of thousands of years, during which the peoples of the Earth outwaited the terrible cold of a global ice age. The word comes from the first line of Ted Hughes's poem *Snowdrop*: 'Now is the world shrunk tight/Round the mouse's dulled wintering heart.'

Wisp – Feathery seeds that move with apparent purpose through the airs of Perth.

Wraith – Wraiths or phantoms are occasionally seen drifting along the roadways of Perth. The folklore of the enclave remains ambiguous as to their nature. Perhaps they are ghosts of the dead, or illusions created by the All Mother. They seem to be sentient because they react to whoever encounters them. The wraiths that Kell meets always remind him of Shamra.

Wrynn – A Thrall Maker but also something of a maverick influence among his kind. He embodies aspects of the Trickster archetype, as does Kell, ensuring his kin do not become too set or complacent in their ways.

Wulfen – A species of the outer world modified from preglacial wolves to survive the ice. Some wulfen packs rely almost solely on their base instincts, while in others intelligence has flourished. This ability to reason has been enhanced by the evolution of a form of telepathy called onemindedness, which allows the individuals in a pack to hunt with the co-ordination of a single animal.

Wulfenhoard – The accumulated wisdom of the wulfen, whose wealth lies in their songs and sagas.

Wulfensweor – Wulf cousin, also used as a term of great respect and affection.

Wulfmaer – A wulf in Magula's pack.

Wyldewulf – 'The one who roams in wild places' and an elder wulf in Magula's pack. Wyldewulf sacrifices himself at the conclusion of *Storm* to save his friends.

Wyrda Craeftum – A tribe of mercenaries united by their unique and startling appearance and their commitment to the Sigel Rad. This translates as 'the sun's way' and represents long-lost knowledge of Man's exploration of space before the Wintering began. The name Wyrda Craeftum means 'with skill given by the Wierds'. This is a reference to the 'loom of fate', a woven predestiny in which the Wyrda and other peoples believe.

Wyrtegemang – A spicy tobacco-like leaf much favoured by the Wyrda Craeftum.

Zauraq – The first warrior of the Wyrda Craeftum whom Alderamin's party meet on the outskirts of Thule. Zauraq, like a number of the Craeftum, earns his keep as a mercenary. Whatever these people do, however, it is only to fulfil their tribe's destiny – a fated path to the stars known as the Sigel Rad or Sun's Way.

A note on the language:
Many of the names, terms and mystical concepts used in The Wintering derive from Anglo-Saxon, Norse and Celtic traditions, although I have adapted them freely to

suit my own purposes. I love the ring and rhythm of these words and wanted to include them to give added texture to the writing. I also wanted to sprinkle the story with words and phrases that at first sight would seem strange, but which might become oddly familiar in the end because they go back to the roots of our language. Logically, the language of people existing thousands of years hence would likely be completely alien to us – much more so than Chaucer's English sounds to the modern ear – but I wanted to create some sense of it having evolved, while (obviously) allowing readers to understand what was being said.

Two books I found especially useful in my 'word weaving' were *The Earliest English Poems*, translated by Michael Alexander, Penguin Classics (1970) and *Wordcraft*, a dictionary and thesaurus of Old English by Stephen Pollington, Anglo Saxon Books (1999).

It may also be of a little interest to you to know that some of the character names and a couple of the place names in The Wintering are based on runes and runic terms. For instance, *Feoh* is a rune signifying ambition satisfied and love fulfilled (according to the writer Ralph Blum): it is used ironically in the story. By contrast, *Kell* comes simply from 'Celtic' because he embodies a number of important beliefs about the cosmos which derive from that culture.

S.B.